HOW TO USE 3,000 YEN

AF621845

By the same author:

Dinner at the Night Library

HOW TO USE 3,000 YEN

HIKA HARADA

Translated by Alison Watts

SCRIBNER

London · New York · Amsterdam/Antwerp · Sydney/Melbourne · Toronto · New Delhi

First published in Great Britain by Scribner, an imprint of
Simon & Schuster UK Ltd, 2026

Copyright © SANZEN-EN NO TSUKAIKATA by Hika Harada 2018
Translation copyright © Alison Watts 2026
Original Japanese edition published by
CHUOKORON-SHINSHA, INC., Japan in 2018
These English rights arranged with
CHUOKORON-SHINSHA, INC. through
The English Agency (Japan) Ltd. and New River Literary Ltd

SCRIBNER and design are registered trademarks of The Gale Group, Inc.,
used under licence by Simon & Schuster Inc.

The right of Hika Harada to be identified as author of this work has been
asserted in accordance with the Copyright, Designs and Patents Act, 1988.

1 3 5 7 9 10 8 6 4 2

Simon & Schuster UK Ltd, 1st Floor, 222 Gray's Inn Road
London WC1X 8HB

For more than 100 years, Simon & Schuster has championed authors and the
stories they create. By respecting the copyright of an author's intellectual property, you
enable Simon & Schuster and the author to continue publishing exceptional
books for years to come. We thank you for supporting the author's copyright
by purchasing an authorized edition of this book.

No amount of this book may be reproduced or stored in any format, nor may it be
uploaded to any website, database, language-learning model, or other repository,
retrieval, or artificial intelligence system without express permission. All rights reserved.
Inquiries may be directed to Simon & Schuster, 222 Gray's Inn Road,
London WC1X 8HB or RightsMailbox@simonandschuster.co.uk

Simon & Schuster Australia, Sydney
Simon & Schuster India, New Delhi

www.simonandschuster.co.uk
www.simonandschuster.com.au
www.simonandschuster.co.in

The authorised representative in the EEA is Simon & Schuster Netherlands BV,
Herculesplein 96, 3584 AA Utrecht, Netherlands. info@simonandschuster.nl

Simon & Schuster strongly believes in freedom of expression and stands against
censorship in all its forms. For more information, visit BooksBelong.com.

A CIP catalogue record for this book is available from the British Library

Trade paperback ISBN: 978-1-3985-2599-3
eBook ISBN: 978-1-3985-2600-6
Audio ISBN: 978-1-3985-3774-3

*This book is a work of fiction. Names, characters, places and incidents are either
a product of the author's imagination or are used fictitiously. Any resemblance
to actual people living or dead, events or locales is entirely coincidental.*

Typeset by M Rules Ltd.
Printed and Bound in the UK using 100% Renewable Electricity at CPI Group (UK) Ltd

FSC
www.fsc.org
MIX
Paper | Supporting
responsible forestry
FSC® C013604

1

How to Use Three Thousand Yen

'How you use three thousand yen can decide your life,' said Miho's grandmother.

'Huh?' Miho Mikuriya lifted her head from the book her nose was buried in. 'What do you mean, it can decide your life?'

'Exactly what I said. What a person does with a small amount like three thousand yen can shape their whole life.' Grandma was sitting at her table sipping tea, while Miho was curled up in a corner reading *Anne of the Island*.

Her grandmother laughed at Miho's bewildered expression. 'That book, for example, when did you buy it?'

'After New Year, with the money you gave me.'

Miho had received exactly ¥3,000 from her grandmother at New Year. She had used it to go to McDonald's with her friends a few times and to buy the book she was now reading.

The money was all gone, but she regretted nothing. She'd had fun with her friends and was still enjoying *Anne of the Island* on her third reading. Though Miho didn't believe she wasted money, it always seemed to disappear too quickly. The same went for her monthly allowance.

'Do you keep a record of how you spend your pocket money?'

'I don't get enough to keep a record.'

Every month she received ¥500 from her parents. This, too, she spent on trips to McDonald's with her friends and buying books. Occasionally, when she ran out, she managed to coax her mother or father into giving her a bit more.

Grandma shook her head, almost as if to say *That's so like you*. 'What about your sister, what did she do with her New Year's money?'

Maho was in high school and Miho was still in middle school, but both had received ¥3,000 from their grandmother.

'Um, what was it ... Oh, I know. She pooled it with her pocket money and got Mum to take her shopping at a department store to buy a pink patent-leather wallet.'

Maho's wallet was cute *and* sophisticated, in Miho's opinion. She knew Maho was looking forward to using it on her school trip.

'So, you spent your money on McDonald's and books, while Maho bought a wallet. Don't you think that says something about each of your characters?'

'Liking books and liking cute things has nothing to do with character,' Miho retorted.

'You'll see,' her grandmother simply muttered.

But Miho didn't believe her. Her life was just beginning, and she couldn't understand why small choices such as what she did with her pocket money would change its course.

'You're so like Marilla, Grandma.'

'What's that?'

'Nothing.'

For some reason, Miho remembered this conversation out of the blue. She was standing in front of a shelf of teapots in a home decor store, when it came back to her with such vividness that she almost dropped the teapot in her hands. Six months earlier, she had moved out of home to live on her own, and in all that time had been using teabags or buying tea at a convenience store on the way to work.

After browsing through the selection, she decided a simple glass pot might be nice. The price was exactly ¥3,000. She could enjoy the colour of both green tea and herbal tea in it, plus, it would go nicely with the white decor she had chosen for her flat.

Miho tried to remember what kind of teapot Maho used. She was fairly sure that Maho had an enamelware coffee pot. Yes ... she could picture it. Maho also used it to boil water, and Miho recalled her carefully washing it so as to avoid scratching the enamel. Maho was five years older than her, and married with a child. She had fallen in love with this pot after seeing it on the Insta feed of a domestic thrift diva she followed, and saved up to buy it. Though Maho had said it was expensive, it still only cost ¥3,980.

Miho's mother used a Scandinavian teapot that her friends

had given her as a birthday present. These were friends she had known since university, which perhaps explained why they were so interested in the latest fashions and food trends in the women's magazines they all read, since the formative years of their youth had been during the economic boom of the late 1980s, or the bubble period as everybody called it.

Miho's grandmother owned a blue-and-white porcelain Royal Copenhagen teapot that she used for black tea, and a handmade pottery one for green tea that she had bought on her travels. Both had been expensive, definitely more than ¥3,000, but she had used them for so many years that a cost-per-day calculation would have to come out at less than ¥3,000 per year.

Whenever Miho thought of her grandmother, she pictured her pouring from one of these teapots, which just went to show how much a part of her everyday life they were. *Now I get it,* she thought. *It's true a person can be defined by how they spend their money.*

Miho returned the glass teapot to the shelf. She wasn't sure that this pot was really her. The transparent glass seemed so fragile and delicate.

For the last few years Miho's life had been entirely focused on graduating from university, finding a job and moving into a place of her own to live.

She worked for a mid-size IT company in West Shinjuku. The IT industry was notorious for the poor working conditions of employees at so-called 'black companies', but Miho's workplace wasn't too bad. Her immediate boss was reasonably open-minded, although his bosses – the company president and executives that made up the core of company management – were reptiles in comparison. The firm had originally been founded as the subsidiary of a subsidiary of a certain telephone company, and changed its name when it split from the parent company ten years previously. It continued, however, to receive business from the government and public corporations, and remained financially stable.

While at university Miho had considered entering various industries, and been torn over which course to choose. She ended up opting for this company because of its energy and vitality, as you might expect from the IT field. Not to mention that it offered solid welfare benefits for employees.

One year after starting there, Miho leased a flat in Yutenji. After growing up on the eastern side of Tokyo in East Jujo, a ten-minute walk from Jujo Station and close to the Jujo Ginza shopping mall, it had been her dream to live on her own in a flat on the western side of Tokyo. She loved living in Yutenji, which was the kind of neighbourhood that estate agents described as a 'quiet residential area'. There was a Blue Bottle Coffee shop nearby and trendy Nakameguro was only five minutes away by bicycle. Including the building service charge, Miho paid ¥98,000 a month in rent for her upscale flat. It was a little expensive, but standard for that part of Tokyo, and she was proud of having found such a good deal on a property of this kind.

In study and in work, Miho always thought carefully about what she wanted before setting out to make her dream come true. All in all, she was pretty satisfied with her life.

Until, that is, Machie Oda was fired.

Forty-four-year-old Machie had been Miho's mentor when she first joined the company. Machie was kind, capable and not at all the hard-nosed go-getter that people in her position often were; rather she had a more unhurried, girlish disposition.

Machie was, in fact, from a very good family. Miho had once been invited to her home in Suginami Ward, where she lived with her mother in a substantial old residence, surrounded by luxuriant shrubbery and high walls. When Miho rang the bell, Machie and her mother both came to the door to welcome her. Machie's mother was petite and quite advanced in years since, unusually for her generation, she had given birth to Machie when she was over thirty-five.

'This place is so old the upkeep is an awful lot of trouble,' Machie said in response to Miho's exclamations of awe. To Miho's ears, Machie sounded sincere and was not simply being modest.

Machie had been wearing the brown-check blouse, brown cardigan and brown skirt that she often wore to work. Miho had also seen her in a navy-blue jacket that she sometimes wore for meetings or visitors, but the word at work was that Machie's dress style had barely changed since she started at the company. She appeared surprisingly indifferent to fashion.

'I'm an only child, and my father passed away early,' she told Miho, showing her into a guest room with a white-covered sofa.

It was clear at a glance that Machie and her mother were a tight-knit unit.

'Mother, Miho brought us a present.'

'Oh my, you shouldn't have.'

'I'm so embarrassed, but since you went to such trouble, would you mind if I served your gift?' Machie said softly.

She's so refined, thought Miho. 'I don't mind if you do!' she responded automatically in an overly loud voice. From her experience of visiting other people's homes in Jujo, she had always thought it polite to say 'No, not at all, I don't mind if you do,' but the volume of her voice might have been out of place here. She felt embarrassed.

Machie and her mother took the cheesecake Miho had bought in Nakameguro out to the kitchen. They returned, giggling as they carried in tea served in an old Japanese teacup patterned with tiny roses, and flanked by the cheesecake and *okaki* rice crackers.

'These are Mother's homemade okaki,' Machie said with a slight blush.

'I dried the New Year's rice cake to make them,' her mother explained, also blushing. 'We get our New Year rice cake from the same shop every year. They always make too much for just the two of us, but it's hard to tell them that we don't need it all.'

'We've known them for ever, you see,' Machie added. 'So we just use the leftovers to make snacks. But I'm overcome with embarrassment at receiving such a lovely gift, Miho.'

'It's nothing. This okaki is delicious!'

The okaki had clearly been carefully prepared in good cooking oil. It was deep-fried, not in the least greasy, and had a light coating of sugar. Although Miho had never eaten okaki before, it had a familiar, nostalgic taste.

'Whenever I have guests over, we always end up serving the same thing.'

'My grandmother makes a good pickled Chinese cabbage that she's always itching to give people,' Miho said.

'Oh, I do envy her. I am utterly hopeless at pickles.'

Watching the two women lean in close and smile at each other, Miho felt like sticking a skewer through all the men at work who speculated about whether Machie was a virgin or not. Machie was liked, and so reliable that people depended on her, but she was also the target of derision.

Earlier in the year, in spring, Machie had suffered a mild stroke. Fortunately, she had been home at the time and was rushed straight to hospital. After a month of being in hospital and then rehabilitation, she was able to return to work. At first, she walked with a slight limp, but this became virtually unnoticeable over a few months. Nonetheless Machie was exempted from doing overtime for quite a while. 'Take it easy, get some rest,' her boss, co-workers and even Miho herself had encouraged her. Machie was grateful and kept up with her rehabilitation therapy.

Miho had been impressed. She found the company's attitude heartening. *This is a good place to work,* she'd thought. *Everybody is so kind.* She was also glad to have confirmation that her judgement in choosing to work here had been spot on.

However, when autumn came and the company embarked on large-scale corporate restructuring, Machie's was the first name to be put forward, and she resigned very quickly after that. After her departure, Miho began experiencing an uncomfortable sense of something being not quite right.

She might be working, eating lunch or in a meeting, when suddenly she would have a flash of memory about Machie. Things Machie had said or taught Miho, the look on her face, or sound of her laughter. Miho's heart felt heavy whenever she tried to imagine what life would be like for Machie now, living in that big old house with her dainty, refined mother.

There were a number of reasons why Machie had been a prime candidate for being pressured into resigning: her work assessment had suffered due to her working fewer hours because of her illness; she was single with no children, and therefore considered 'easy to let go'; she lived in a large house – albeit one that belonged to her mother – and everybody knew she came from a good family in upscale Suginami Ward; and she drew a large salary despite not being in a managerial position, because she was a university graduate who had worked for the company for many years.

Was it really possible that someone – anyone – should have to leave for those reasons?

Machie's mother had been in good health when Miho met her, but was at an age when she might very well soon require nursing care. And, as everybody knew, it would be difficult for Machie to find another job since she was over forty.

The day after Machie's departure, Miho found herself staring at the empty desk opposite. It felt as if the ground beneath her feet had shifted. Everything that had once made her feel confident and secure had been swept away, to be replaced with uncertainty. She looked at her bosses and colleagues laughing as they played air golf in the office during their break. *They don't care a fig about Machie,* she thought, *it all goes on just the same for them.* She couldn't understand why this thought depressed her so much. But had she been asked what else could have been done instead, she would have had no answer. Miho knew that she was not willing to put herself forward in place of Machie as a candidate to be laid off. Even if it would be much easier for her, being younger, to find another job than it was for Machie. More and more, Miho found herself coming to resent the company for making her feel this way.

December arrived and with it the season for year-end parties. Naturally, Miho's workplace had them, too. The main event was a big dinner attended by about two hundred department managers and their subordinates, which then split into smaller section-based groups for a round of after-parties. The task of organising this evening always fell to the newest and youngest employees, still in their early twenties. It was a particularly arduous time of year for them, as all the parties they were required to attend and organise left them feeling drop-dead exhausted.

Miho had also had a tough time the previous year when she was an organiser for the first time. But Machie had offered her help, the sole senior staff member willing to do so, and it was only thanks to Machie that Miho managed at all. Every year, Machie supported and encouraged the newest employees in this way, both openly and behind the scenes, helping them with the unfamiliar task of organising such a large-scale event, giving advice when asked, and checking that nothing had been overlooked at the end.

As she recalled this while in the midst of preparations for this year's event, Miho was almost brought to a standstill by tears and emotion. She was in no doubt that without Machie's help last year she could not have survived, and was deeply grateful to Machie for all she had been taught. This year, Miho was doing her best to help the newest members of the company as much as possible.

On the day of the party, the main dinner went off without a hitch, then everybody moved on to karaoke bars for the after-parties. Miho had reserved a large room in a karaoke club which could accommodate everyone from her section. She broke the ice by singing a duet with her section chief, so that those bosses who actually did want to sing, but were reluctant to put themselves forward first, could then get started. Once this duty was done, everybody jostled for a turn, as if it were a competition. Miho left them to it and went to sit down in a corner of the room. She had barely eaten anything at the dinner because she had been too busy mixing drinks for her boss, stirring the hotpots and serving up the food, and was relieved at last to be able to partake of the cold pizza and fries. Then she heard a low voice nearby.

'So, did Department Head Minamiyama fuck her in the end?'

Miho didn't catch the whole conversation, but could tell immediately what kind of exchange this was: someone stabbing somebody else in the back. The vulgar tone made her want to cover her ears with both hands.

'You gotta be kidding. At least that's what he said. Doubt if he'd sink so low.'

Miho heard suppressed sniggering, and looked around circumspectly to see five or six of the bosses in her group, huddled close in a corner as they drank and slung mud. The subject of their conversation, Mr Minamiyama the department head, was happily singing karaoke. The group observed him as they drank.

'Is Machie still a virgin then?'

'Have to be, I reckon.'

Miho instantly felt her blood drain as she realised they were talking about Machie. Her fingers went cold.

'Damnit. To think I was tiptoeing around her because the rumour is she's Minamiyama's woman.'

'You had it wrong. He didn't even speak up for her when she was let go.'

'That figures.'

'Maybe he didn't defend her *because* of that rumour.'

'In any case, she always did take advantage of her authority to boss people around like she owned the place.'

'Once someone gets like that it's hard for them to make it in the outside world,' said Section Chief Kato with inexplicable feeling. He was Machie's senior by two years.

'She wasn't too bad at her job, and upper management paid her a lot of attention, so I guess she got the wrong idea somehow. It's not as if she could pull that off in another position or company.'

Miho was sickened by their patronising criticism, cloaked with a veneer of eminent reasonableness and sympathy.

'Put like that it makes her seem like a victim of the company, somehow,' another section chief, younger than Machie, said in a knowing tone.

'She had it coming,'

Miho couldn't identify this speaker. She couldn't bear it any more and stood up to go to the bathroom, but all of a sudden was overcome by nausea, as if she had eaten too much. Her stomach heaved and she promptly vomited up its entire contents.

'What a waste. That's too bad,' said Daiki Hasegawa, putting down his coffee cup after hearing Miho's story.

December had been so busy that Miho and Daiki, her boyfriend, had not been able to see each other for quite some time. When they did eventually meet on Christmas Eve, before she knew it Miho found herself telling Daiki everything that had happened. 'After all Machie's done for the company, hearing them talk like that made me wonder what point there was in trying my best there.'

Daiki's eyeballs moved in his head as he concentrated on picking out his words. 'Once you start thinking about the meaning of work and life, of course it's gonna make you feel hopeless. Anyone, not just young people like us, but the older guys in the company as well.'

'I don't know about that.'

'We're all just little people. That's why those guys were so into talking shit like that. They feel insecure, and talk big to match each other. It's important to recognise that, at least. But you, Miho, you're amazing, because you're not afraid to face up to your own smallness, or weaknesses.'

Ah, now I remember, Miho thought, *Daiki was always like this. So kind, and good at consoling me.* He was adept at bolstering

Miho who, though she might not come across that way, was less robust in her thoughts and easily disheartened. She remembered why she'd fallen in love with him.

'Besides, I think there's some truth in what they said.'

'What?'

A chill wind intruded on Miho's touching appreciation of Daiki's kindness.

'Machie could have had a side to her that you never saw.'

'No way. Machie isn't like that. But anyway, what would you do if you happened to get caught up in a conversation like that at work?'

'I guess I'd probably just keep quiet, smile and listen, even if I didn't contribute. Gossip is one of society's necessary evils. And gossip like that about women who aren't on a management career track especially, doesn't hurt or bother anyone.'

Management career track? All of a sudden Daiki was sounding middle-aged in Miho's ears. 'That's disgusting.'

'No, it's not. Was it really so bad what those guys said?'

Miho felt a small, but very real shock, as if she had been slapped in the face. She glared at Daiki.

'You speak highly of Machie, but from what you say it sounds like all she did was grease the wheels in the workplace. I haven't heard anything that indicates she was involved in any kind of core sales work for the company. Can you really call that being talented at your job? There's a woman at work who lords it over everybody, just because she's been there a long time, but to be honest, I think she's an eyesore. Wouldn't surprise me if management decided she wasn't needed any more. Things might have been different in the bubble era, but these days companies can't afford to keep on people like that.'

Can't afford to keep ... Miho's heart froze at his choice of words.

'In any case, it can't be helped. There's nothing you can do, Miho.'

This last utterance made Miho smart. 'So, Daiki, if somebody said about me what they did about Machie, would that be okay with you?'

'That wouldn't happen to you, Miho. You'll probably get married someday, have kids and quit your job like normal people do.'

What? Marriage? Someday? What did Daiki mean? At another time, these words might have set her heart pounding, but this was different. Miho had had no inkling that Daiki's thinking was so old-fashioned. She stared at him in astonishment, while he averted his eyes as if to avoid her gaze.

'I'm not so irresponsible as to start a job, intending to quit as soon as I get married. It's different nowadays, most women want to try and keep their jobs, even after having children.'

'Well, work all you like then.'

Miho felt as if she had been dismissed. As if Daiki had told her that his life and hers couldn't compare. Oblivious to her agitation, Daiki changed the subject and began talking about a new project at work.

Over the New Year period, Miho went to stay with her parents in Jujo. Her mother had sent an email with an insistent plea for her to come home early and help with the annual housecleaning and preparation of *osechi*, the traditional New Year's dishes. However, as soon as work finished on the 27th, Miho left for a skiing trip with some friends from university and did not arrive back in Tokyo until the night of the 30th. The next day she awoke around noon, and it was close to evening before she arrived at her parents' house.

'Miho, you're late. What've you been doing?' came her mother's voice when she opened the door, but not sounding as cross as the words might suggest, and for some reason laced with laughter.

'Hi there,' Miho responded sullenly, not answering the question. In addition to the guilt she felt for not helping, she was annoyed at being laughed at.

'We're all done, Miho,' her older sister Maho piled on in a cheerful tone. 'There's nothing left for you to do.'

Maho's three-year-old daughter, Saho, raced to the door. 'Miho nuffing,' she lisped, in imitation of her mother.

Miho knew that her adored niece did not actually understand what she was saying, but she was feeling frayed and irritable. 'You won't get any New Year money from me if you say things like that, Saho,' she said with a scowl.

'Miho scary, scary!'

Miho followed Saho as she trotted back to Maho in the kitchen-dining room and buried her face in her mother's chest. Miho's grandmother, mother and Maho were seated around the table, which groaned under the weight of all the food they had prepared. Their upturned faces looking in Miho's direction all bore a strong resemblance to each other, despite Miho's paternal grandmother and mother not being related by blood. To Miho's eyes, the large round faces and small, pouty lips of each, seated on either side of Maho, made them seem like beans that could have sprung from the same pod. That included her own face, which she was tired of seeing in the mirror every morning.

'Really, Miho, don't be so childish,' her mother scolded, with a scowl ten times scarier than Miho's earlier.

'Welcome home.' Only Miho's grandmother greeted her as usual.

'Hi, Grandma.'

'You're too late. The cleaning's done, and we've almost finished preparing the food.'

'I told you I was going skiing.'

'Oh really, you're always the same. All you do is eat, and never help with the cleaning. I was going to get you to do the bathtub and rain shutters,' Miho's mother added.

'But I told you.' Miho knew it was a waste of time arguing. She went over to the sofa in the adjoining living-room area and plopped herself down.

'Stay here, you could at least do one thing.'

'All right. I could puree sweet potato for the *kinton*, or the two-coloured egg.' Both these dishes were standards on the Mikuri family's osechi menu, and even Miho, who was not a good cook, knew how to make them. Helping prepare the osechi dishes for New Year was equivalent to pureeing food for her. But she found both the work itself and the ritual of it boring. It was a mystery to her why her mother, grandmother and recently Maho too, threw themselves into it with such enthusiasm.

'We've finished both.'

'What about the kelp rolls then? I could roll the herring in kelp and tie the dried gourd?'

'Maho's doing that now.'

'Well, I could twist pieces of *konnyaku* jelly for the chicken and vegetable stew.'

In the order of things, once the pureeing was done, next came the work of rolling, and then twisting.

'Finished.'

'What about peeling yams?'

'Did that yesterday.'

'Cutting the carrots into flowers?'

'Your sister did that for me.'

'Cooking the black beans?'

'That's the only thing left, but we can't let you do it.'

Miho didn't fully understand why, but for some reason having simmered black beans with no wrinkles in the skin was a top priority for her mother and grandmother. Every year they tried out all sorts of methods in search of perfect, unwrinkled beans. During these family gatherings, Miho's mother and grandmother behaved as if they were the best of friends. But sometimes, when Miho overheard her mother speaking to her own mother on the phone in dialect, she became aware that her mother was in fact very careful around her mother-in-law. Knowing how much her daughters adored their grandmother, Miho's mother never spoke ill of her, but their relationship was clearly not the same as a real mother and daughter's.

'This year,' her mother said, 'we got back to basics and did it the old-fashioned way. No pressure cooker, just let the sugar soak slowly into the beans. They've been steeping in sugar water for three days now—'

'What about kneading pureed sweet potatoes for the *kinton*?' Miho cut in, afraid that her mother would not stop once she started talking about beans.

'You did that the year before last, but you burned it, didn't you? I can't ask you again. I'll do it this year.'

'So, what's left then?'

'Seasoning the stewed chicken and vegetables, simmered soybeans with vegetable and shrimp, and grilling the prawns and sea bream. Then arranging it all in the serving boxes, but I can't have you do any of that.'

'So, there's nothing for me to do, right?'

'Well, you were late, weren't you?'

Whatever Miho said, they went round in circles. She flopped down on the sofa in a sulk.

'You could play with Saho.'

'All right then.'

Miho swivelled her neck to look in Saho's direction but the little girl, who ordinarily would be all over Miho, was still smarting from the earlier scowl and stuck close to her mother, refusing to be parted.

'Go and have a rest, Miho. You must be tired since you work all the time,' her grandmother said gently.

'You always spoil Miho, Grandma. I'm tired too, from doing housework and looking after a child,' Maho protested loudly.

Miho closed her ears and pretended to doze. The three women soon went back to their work and chat. *They don't really care whether I'm here or not,* Miho thought, *it makes no difference to them.* The osechi dishes are all ready and the cleaning finished – the house is always spotless anyway since Mum loves cleaning so much. She heard Maho asking for advice on where to look for work once Saho started kindergarten. She couldn't find anything suitable, and let slip that her husband's salary was low. Miho did not really believe that her sister was in financial trouble. If she truly didn't have enough to put food on the table, she would take any kind of work, wouldn't she? Presumably her grandmother and mother knew that, too, which is why they listened to Maho without comment.

Miho knew she shouldn't think it, but she did wonder how Maho could marry someone who earned only ¥230,000 a month, and then go and have a baby as well. Her brother-in-law, Taiyo, was a firefighter; a good-looking guy with tanned skin and white teeth. He and Maho had been together since high school and married as soon as Taiyo started working. Maho went to junior college and then got a job in a securities firm, but quit that when she married.

I couldn't imagine marrying someone who makes slightly over three million a year, let alone quitting my job right away and having children. Why am I so mean? My brother-in-law is a good man, who has a stable income because he works for the government. And Saho is cute, too – Taiyo even cried when Saho was born, because he was so moved. And yet . . .

'Auntie, what's wrong? Are you awake?' asked Saho, peering into Miho's face.

'Quit calling me Auntie, just say Miho.'

Saho squealed and ran off giggling. Though only three

years old, she knew that calling Miho 'Auntie' was a sure way to press her button.

'Hey!' Miho jumped up from the sofa to chase after Saho. Thrilled at the reaction, Saho raced around the house chortling loudly.

Miho suddenly wondered if, maybe, she was in pursuit of a happiness that was elusive and way beyond her reach.

Miho found it hard going staying with her parents, and ended up lying that she had work to do so she could leave after two days. Upon arriving back at Yutenji Station, she was surprised to find that the bakery she always went to was open during the New Year period. *It just goes to show how many other people there are in the area who are single like me, don't go home to their parents and need bread at this time of year,* she thought. She bought sandwich bread and a snack bun with walnuts and figs to take back to her flat.

When she opened the front door, Miho let out a long sigh of relief. The sound of her own voice surprised her: *It wasn't like this when I first left home. Even though I wanted to live on my own, I still went back every weekend, and would always call Mum at any small noise in the night that scared me.*

It wasn't so long ago that Miho had still felt secure in the knowledge that she could return to her parents' house any time she needed. But at some point, she had stopped going back, and hadn't been there in several months before New Year. Was her parents' house no longer her permanent home, perhaps?

Miho immediately ran a bath and added her favourite bath

salts. She scrubbed herself all over, then submerged herself in the water to slowly warm up.

After the bath she went to the fridge and found the red wine left over from Christmas. She poured a glass to have with her fig bun. The cold but delicious wine prompted another heartfelt sigh. This was the wine she had drunk with Daiki on Christmas Eve, for an evening that had turned out so flat they didn't even finish the bottle. At least they had found the time to be together, but all they had done was eat dinner at an underwhelming restaurant, exchange presents – Miho had received a small necklace while she gave Daiki a fountain pen worth about ¥10,000 – and then come back to Miho's flat where they watched a film streamed from the internet.

Still, I do like living here, Miho thought, comforted by the taste of her fig bun and red wine.

Just over a week later, Miho was walking through Nakameguro on Coming-of-Age Day, which was a public holiday. Nakameguro was the kind of place that people went to in couples or groups, especially around the Meguro River area, where there were cafés and restaurants run by popular male idols, thronging with female fans. It was not the kind of place where it was cool to be alone, but Miho was alone. Daiki was busy, and her only interaction with him since the end of last year had been an exchange of LINE messages and phone calls.

However, this was of little concern to her. She was aware that her feelings for Daiki had cooled, and for the last six months had been wondering if perhaps their relationship had run its course. It was one of those things that couldn't be helped, she believed. As they worked for different companies, then their respective values and positions would change. Daiki used to be more understanding about women working, and she found it hard to believe that he could now say the things he did. Maybe it was a sign he wasn't interested in her any more.

Wuff! A small bark stopped Miho in her tracks, and she turned to look. *Wuff! Wuff!* it came again, followed immediately by high-pitched yelping, almost as if to say: *Here, look at me!* She was at the front of Nakameguro Station, where the buses and taxis stopped, outside a building alongside which was a small space lined with food stalls. This was where she spotted him – a Chihuahua with a black back, staring up at her with his little eyes wide open. Next to him was a large, white dog that seemed more placid. Miho studied the scene, and realised this was a booth run by a volunteer group trying to find homes for rescue dogs and cats. There was a photo display of the dogs and cats needing homes, and a line of tins for donations. It was a far more unassuming set-up than the surrounding stalls selling freshly grilled sausages and direct-produce vegetables. But the animals' appeal more than made up for this. Miho was riveted. She moved towards the dogs, as if drawn, and crouched down.

'Hello! We're Shine Angels, a volunteer group for rescue dogs and cats,' a woman with a kindly face said. She wore a natural beige shirt and khaki trousers, and had her hair pulled back.

'Are these two rescue dogs?' Miho stroked the big dog so it could have a fair share of attention, too.

The Chihuahua yapped jealously and the big dog observed it tenderly.

'They're being cared for in our shelter for now.'

'I can't believe a Chihuahua would be in a shelter.'

'Yes, we rescued this one from the Public Health dog pound.'

'How old is it?'

'We can't say for certain, but perhaps around five.'

The Chihuahua rubbed its head on Miho's knees as she knelt.

'Such a cute dog – I don't understand.'

Miho had long been aware of the issue of abandoned dogs, having watched a TV documentary and seen it discussed on Twitter, but this was the first time she'd seen evidence of it with her own eyes. She had assumed they were mostly mongrels, or large dogs, or elderly dogs needing special care. She had nothing but admiration for the volunteers who tried to do something for them, as it was not something she felt capable of doing. But the sight of these dogs moved her. Maybe she *could* look after a young, healthy dog.

'I know how you feel,' the woman replied. 'Do you like dogs?'

'I had one when I was little . . .' Miho's heart ached at the thought, and she couldn't say any more.

'Are you able to keep a pet in the place you live now?'

'No, it's a rented flat.'

'That would be difficult,' the woman said. She handed Miho a pamphlet. 'There will be other dogs and cats. You can also always see the latest information on our website. Please have a look.'

'Thank you.'

'We have various conditions you must meet in order to adopt a rescue dog or cat, but if you meet the requirements there are always animals in need of a new home. If it ever becomes possible for you to adopt one, please get in touch.'

'Thank you.' Miho asked if she could pick the Chihuahua up for a hug. The warmth of its tiny body surprised her and it stared intently into her eyes as she held it.

Ever since her encounter with the rescue dogs, Miho had not been able to get them out of her mind. As a child she had had a miniature dachshund called Pea, short for peanut because he had been the same shape and colour as a peanut when he was a puppy. He had been her heart's treasure. But one day, when she was in middle school and Pea was more than ten years old, he disappeared. There had been omens. As Pea got older, he had become confused a lot of the time, then one rainy day he went out of the house and never came back. Miho was heartbroken.

She had yearned to have a dog and pleaded repeatedly with her parents to get one. Eventually they gave in and she promised to look after the dog its whole life, but once she went to middle school and became busy with study, club activities and friends, she had left Pea's care up to her parents. Whenever Miho went out, Pea would stare at her mournfully from a corner of the room. Maybe he was smart enough to understand that his humans were quarrelling over him, or maybe he thought he was unloved, Miho could not be sure which, but even now she felt her chest tighten whenever she recalled those eyes.

Miho did her best to find Pea, but never succeeded. Later, she learned the cruel truth: Pea had apparently ended up in the Public Health dog pound and was put down after the owner failed to come forward. She blamed herself for not thinking to look there at the time, and had never forgiven herself. Taking in a rescue dog now might be a way – just a little – of making amends. Perhaps coming to the aid of a rescue dog who had been in the same position as Pea could become her new purpose and goal in life.

Back at home Miho checked the volunteer group's website, and was astonished by how many dogs were listed there. She found a photo of the Chihuahua she had just met, along with many other small dogs. When she caught herself looking at the younger, cuter dogs, she felt so ashamed that she almost shut off the page. *But if I'm going to keep a dog for many years, of course it makes sense to choose one that I like the look of, and seems compatible.* Such were the excuses that Miho told herself as she continued looking.

She recalled the woman from Shine Angels mentioning that there were conditions for prospective owners, and clicked on the page *Considering Adopting a Pet*, to see what these were. First, the owner had to be willing to pay for the animal to be vaccinated and neutered. Second, was that all pets had to be kept inside, and in order to confirm this, volunteers would bring the animals directly to their new homes. Third, adoptive carers must find someone to sign a statement guaranteeing that they would take care of the pet in the event that the new owner became unable to, due to illness or death etc. There were all sorts of other stipulations but these three were the main ones.

It was a lot more stringent than Miho had expected. However, she realised it was also a sign of the seriousness with which Shine Angels cared for the animals.

Immediately, Miho began to search for pet-friendly flats in her area. Predictably, the few she found were eye-wateringly expensive; almost all being double her current rent. It was clear that she could not afford one on her salary, and even if she did pull out all the stops to rent one, if she were to be laid off for some reason or had to take a pay cut, she would be out on the street with a dog. No – this was not an option, it was too much to put onto herself and an inexcusable thing to do to a dog. She could not call herself a reliable candidate for adopting a rescue dog.

Then Miho had another thought: the conditions for prospective owners written on this page were just as applicable to herself as to a rescue dog. She needed a suitable dwelling, a healthy body and, of course, money. Regardless of whether or not she adopted a dog, these were all necessary.

As far as housing went, she had recently finally come to the realisation that her parents' house was not her permanent home any more, and she also had no immediate plans for marriage. And as for work, well, until recently her sense of security in life had been pinned to the company she worked for, but Machie's departure had shown her the uncertainty of this. She was not, actually, in a stable place at all. Her position as it was might be fine during her twenties, but once she became older, she could be discarded – just like that.

How are you going to live from now on? the little dogs silently staring out at Miho from the screen seemed to ask. Would she be able to find another, more secure, and if possible, better-paid job? She knew that such jobs were difficult to find without having done the hard study at university for the requisite qualifications. To be a doctor, for example, or nurse or lawyer. It was unrealistic to think she could do anything like that. And besides, it wasn't what she wanted to do anyway.

When it came down to it, she concluded, the only way was to accumulate security in small stages, working towards it one step at a time. Miho stared at all the photos of small dogs.

What was possible for her now?

Could she buy a pet-friendly flat or house? She had heard of women buying flats when they were young, but Miho had always thought that this was out of her league. In trepidation, she opened another page on her computer. Maybe it was out of the question, but she needed to know *how much* out of the question.

Entering *Meguro Ward + second-hand flat* into the search engine, she pressed the key and looked at the results. Sigh. There was nothing to even list. Next, she tried *Suginami Ward + second-hand flat, Yokohama + Toyoko line + second-hand flat, Taito Ward + second-hand flat, Setagaya Ward + second-hand houses.* Her search continued late into the night, until dawn.

'So, what happened? You did a complete about-turn and started saving like crazy?'

The following month, Miho was at her sister's flat in Jujo where Maho lived with her family. *You should come over for dinner sometime,* Maho had texted her. She had sent Miho several such invitations since New Year, giving Miho the idea that maybe Maho, too, was not happy with the way things had ended somewhat awkwardly then. Her sister might play the ditzy housewife, but Miho knew her to be considerate and mindful. It was typical of her to write, *Taiyo's working on Sunday so come on over – I'll be lonely*, making it look like Miho would be doing her a favour. Miho knew Maho was making it easy for her, so after repeated invitations, she was ready to go. But she decided that she would not be dropping in to her parents' house nearby while she was there.

Maho's three-roomed flat was, as usual, clean and tidy. The hamburger steak with spaghetti sauce that she served for lunch was unpretentious fare typical of a family with children, but the hamburger meat was juicy and delicious. Miho was also impressed by the homemade apple cake that Maho served for dessert. Seated around the table like this, just hanging out and taking it easy, there was none of the awkwardness from New Year, and Miho was conscious of the sisterly bond between them. She had just told Maho about her search for a house where could keep a pet, and efforts to save money for that purpose.

'Wow, Mi-chan, I can't believe you want to buy not just a property, but a house at that, not a flat. Good for you – that's amazing. We'll probably be renting a flat our whole lives, let alone ever think about buying a house.'

Before lunch Saho had been bouncing around noisily but had fallen asleep obediently as soon as she had eaten. The sisters conversed in low voices to make the most of the small window of time before Saho awoke.

'A house might be a less realistic goal than a flat,' Maho said.

In reply, Miho showed her the search screen of her smartphone. 'Flats are more popular than houses, which means houses are cheaper. Of course it depends on the location.'

Maho exclaimed in surprise.

'Besides, you also have to think about regular maintenance and building fund payments for flats, so once you take those into consideration buying a house might be a better option.'

'But you have to manage the upkeep of a house yourself. Which seems to be quite expensive and time-consuming. At least, Mother is always going on about the maintenance costs at home.'

Trust a housewife to think of those details, thought Miho. 'Maybe so. But look at this property,' she countered, showing Maho a house going for about ten million in the outer suburbs. 'This one with a garden is 10.38 million. I might be able to buy something at this price one day.'

'Loans for second-hand places are usually more difficult to get,' Maho came back.

Once again, Miho was impressed by her sister's grasp of the overall picture and wealth of financial knowledge. She reminded herself that Maho had worked for a securities firm before her marriage. 'That's why I'm trying hard to save money,' she said. 'Also, prices might go down once the Tokyo Olympics are over.'

At this, Maho gave a big smile and nodded. 'I'm relieved to hear you taking a long-term view. You really do mean it.'

'Of course I do.'

'I thought it might be a passing phase. But pets and houses are lifelong commitments. There are responsibilities.'

'I know that.'

The rescue dog may have been the trigger that set Miho thinking about how to save and economise, but the ground had already been prepared for her to rethink her life after the incident with Machie and disagreements with Daiki. Finding the dog was a spark that lit the fire.

Miho drank the second cup of tea her sister poured from the lovely enamel pot that she remembered.

'Well, you'll need to save ten million.'

Miho gasped.

'If you're going to buy a house without a loan, you have to save at least that much first.'

Ten million yen. *It's true,* Miho thought, *I might need that much.* It was a figure she had not seriously reckoned with so far.

'Our goal is also to save ten million. We have Saho's education to think of.'

'What? Are you serious? You're thinking that, too? How much have you saved?' Miho burst out, then clamped her mouth shut, realising it was the kind of question you might not want to ask even a sister. In fact, Maho being her sister might be even more reason not to ask. 'Sorry, you don't have to say if you don't want.'

'Right now, we have a little over six million,' Maho replied without hesitation.

'What?' Miho gasped. How could Maho have saved so much when she had only been married for six years, her husband made ¥3 million a year, *and* they had a child?

'I had one million saved before we married, and Taiyo

didn't have anything. But I was able to bring it up to a little over six million by putting around a third in a fluctuating investment trust. I couldn't save more because we had a lot of expenses the year Saho was born,' Maho hurried to explain, taking Miho's surprise the wrong way.

'No, no you've got it wrong. I can't believe you saved so much. Almost a million yen a year, right? How did you do it?'

If Maho can do it, I can save ten million in ten years too, Miho thought. She didn't say this out loud, because she knew that her own salary was higher than her brother-in-law's. And she had no children or spouse to support. Miho looked down at the table again. 'Don't tell me you usually only eat tofu and bean sprouts. And today you went overbudget to bake me a cake?'

Maho laughed and looked smug. 'Don't worry. It's always like this. We don't eat fancy food, but I spend about twenty thousand yen a month on groceries.'

'What!' This was Miho's second surprise of the day.

'I'm single, but I spend thirty to forty thousand yen a month on food.'

'It's the other way round – because you're single you spend that much. When you work, it's much harder to cook for yourself, right?'

'But *how* do you save so much?' Miho sighed deeply. 'To be honest I've been trying to save, too, but it's hopeless. Last month I tried to cook for myself, and bought a bunch of stuff. But when I did the calculations at the end of the month, it turned out I'd spent more than usual. Actually, I don't have a full-enough grasp of how much I was spending to begin with, but I do know I was in the red.'

Wasn't that the truth. In an effort to save money, Miho had gone shopping at the supermarket. She had decided to start making her own lunch and so she bought an artisan-crafted bento box made of natural cedar that cost ¥8,000. But the lunch-making effort didn't last more than a day, and she hadn't been able to consume all the ingredients she'd bought, ending up having to throw most away. To save on electricity, she refrained from using the heater and showered instead of having a bath. The chill she felt as a result might have contributed to her catching a cold and needing to see a doctor. The guilt she felt from wasting food was so stressful that she ended up eating out more and more. So now, she was feeling down, wondering if she would ever be able to cook for herself.

'Miho, how much money *do* you have saved?'

Miho was silent for a few beats. 'Three hundred thousand . . . Maybe.'

'What? Is that all?' Maho stared hard at her. 'In that case you need to thoroughly reorganise, don't you? How about reviewing your fixed costs? Start saving on outgoing sums.'

'Fixed costs?'

'Things like rent, or smartphone plans – costs that are absolutely essential.'

'But if they are literally "fixed costs", then I can't change them, can I?'

'Reviewing food and electricity bills won't amount to much. It's easiest to economise by cutting fixed costs first.'

This made Miho pause for thought. Her place in Yutenji was comfortable and she liked it a lot. She was proud of living there.

'You pay ninety-eight thousand yen in rent. That's too much,' said Maho. 'Groceries would be expensive in that area too. I bet the supermarkets are all the fancy, pricey type of place.'

'I guess so,' Miho replied.

'Of course they are. Come and live here. In Jujo. It's closer to Shinjuku this side, and rent is ten to twenty thousand yen cheaper. Also, how much do you spend on your smartphone?'

'About ten thousand a month.'

'So much! I pay two thousand. I can make as many ten-minute calls as I want.'

'No!'

Maho showed Miho her smartphone. It was a pink, rather cute device.

'Is that one of those super-cheap-deal phones?'

'Yeah. And even cheaper because I got extra discount in a campaign. See, if you reduce your rent by twenty thousand and smartphone by eight thousand, you can start saving almost thirty thousand a month, right away.'

'Jujo, huh?'

'Jujo's nothing to sniff at. It has good, cheap food and plenty of low-price supermarkets. You could eat at Mum and Dad's sometimes, too, and Mum would probably give you food from time to time.'

'Isn't that a bit …' *Sneaky*, Miho didn't say, not to mention she had declared herself to be independent of home.

'They'd be pleased. We go there once a week, too, and Mum gives me all kinds of stuff. Grandma is nearby and we also visit. They get to see their grandchildren and great-grandchildren too – win-win for everyone.'

'Uh-huh.'

'Or better yet, go and live at home! You could pay thirty thousand a month to Mum and Dad, and save the rest! You should do it!'

'No way!'

Dejected, Miho slumped down on the table. She knew her sister was right about every single thing.

After a while, Maho spoke again. 'Why don't you start with saving a hundred yen a day.'

'A hundred yen?' Was Maho making fun of her? Implying that this was all that Miho was capable of?

'You could save a hundred yen on tea or coffee, or whatever you spend on sweets at the convenience store, right? Do that for a month and you have three thousand yen. Then you put that into an investment fund every month.'

'An investment fund? Through a bank?'

'You can do it at a bank, but you should open an account at a brokerage firm. I recommend an indexed fund with as few charges as possible. When you have three thousand yen, bring it to me. I'll show you how. Ah – you should also get advice before opening a brokerage account. Some places will pay a fee to anyone who introduces a new customer.' Maho gave a satisfied smile. 'I can make a mini-profit,' she murmured, using a term Miho was not familiar with.

'Gotcha. I'll buy a piggy bank on my way home.'

'Idiot. How is that going to help save money?'

Miho hadn't been called 'idiot' in a long time, but it didn't bother her the way it used to when she was a child, in fact she felt nostalgic. And most importantly, she knew that she was not alone.

'Can I buy something from a hundred-yen store?'

'You can't do that either. Save the hundred yen.'

Maho went to rummage through the kitchen shelves and pulled out a small tin with a lid. 'Here, this was a souvenir can of nuts from a friend who went to Hawaii. Use this for your piggy bank.'

At this point, Saho awoke from her nap, putting an end to any further complicated discussion. Miho thanked her sister and went home.

One hundred yen a day – I can do that. Miho's feelings had been ruffled while talking with Maho, but she had to admit it was an achievable goal.

She was giving this more thought the next morning, while sipping on the latest flavour of Frappuccino from the Seattle-based coffee shop she regularly stopped off at on her way to work. Every day she got up early in order to drop by this coffee shop near her office and plan her day. She looked forward to this part of her daily routine, and the boost of energy it gave her for the coming day. Normally, she would go to a convenience store next to buy a bottled drink before heading to work, but not today. Today she had brought her tea in a thermos mug. This would free up ¥150. Still a long way off ¥10 million, though.

The ¥150 in coins that she dropped into the can her sister had given her made a satisfying clink. Miho intended to put this on her desk at work, and save up little by little. However, she still hadn't come to any decision as to how she would cut her fixed costs, as Maho had suggested. The two-year contract on her smartphone was due to expire in six months, and she was amenable to changing it then. *I think I'll do that,* she decided. She did have some concerns about using a super-cheap smartphone, but was willing to put up with a slightly tacky older model for the sake of rescuing a cute little dog. But what about her rent? It had always been her dream to live on the western side of Tokyo. And wouldn't it be like some kind of . . . Miho searched for the word – defeat . . . to move home, or somewhere nearby? She couldn't shake the feeling that moving back would be a sign of failure.

'No, it's not like that. Akabane is right next to Jujo, and ranked one of the most popular areas to live now!' Maho had told her.

Miho thought about what else she could do to save. *I know – I can read books about economising, and go to seminars! Think of all I learned from just talking to Maho, an amateur, so if I went to an expert, I might get even better advice.*

Having travelled thus far in her train of thought, Miho slurped down the last of her Frappuccino. It tasted weak. She had only drunk about half, but the ice had completely melted, turning it into nothing more than a weak, sweet coffee drink. *This always happens,* she thought. *I can never drink a whole Frappuccino while it still tastes good . . . Maybe this coffee is a waste of money!* She checked the price again. Until now she had never paid much attention to cost since she always paid with the shop's original pre-paid card, but the cheapest Frappuccino here cost ¥420 (before tax), a plain iced coffee ¥280 (before tax), while an iced coffee at a convenience store was ¥100 . . . Until this moment, Miho had believed there to be no great differences in the price of coffee. *What's a difference of a hundred yen here and there,* had been her attitude. *I might as well drink what I like.* But if she was going to save ¥100 every day, well, that was a different story. She didn't want to stop going to coffee shops, but if all she was doing was making time for herself to think, then an iced coffee would suffice. *I'll get iced coffee every second day,* she decided.

'Is this seat taken?'

Miho looked up to see a young guy in casual college clothes pointing at the seat next to her. The auditorium had been mostly empty when she arrived but now, nearly a full five minutes before the talk was due to begin, almost all the seats were filled.

'No, feel free,' she said, moving her bag off the seat. 'Sorry about that.' She would not have called him handsome, but he did strike her as clean-cut and fresh in appearance.

Miho was attending a seminar given by financial planner and adviser on economising Suko Kurofune, whose book *8 x 12 Is the Magic Number* was a recent bestseller. Miho had not actually read the book, but she happened to hear about it on TV, and came across details for the seminar when searching for more information online. The attendance fee was a low ¥3,000, to celebrate publication of the new book, and the subtitle of today's talk also appealed to Miho: *Dedicated to men and women in their twenties and thirties, especially salaried workers and college students about to enter the workforce.* This was more her thing, as frankly she did not believe that studying economising techniques for housewives would be of great use to her.

Ms Kurofune made a dashing entrance onto the stage after

a brief introduction from the moderator. She was around the same age as Miho's mother, and plump – plumper than she looked on TV, which was unusual since TV usually made people appear fatter than in real life, not the other way round.

'Everybody, I want you to remember this.' Launching straight in, without so much as a word of greeting, Ms Kurofune grabbed a pen to write on the whiteboard. *8 x 12*, she wrote large, just like the title of her book.

'This is all you need to remember from now on. Just this. I want you to imprint it in your brains. Now, what does eight times twelve come to?'

'Ninety-six!' a voice from the audience shouted.

'Yes. That is correct. You will save eighty thousand yen every month, and an additional twenty thousand every bonus time. Then, wonder of wonders, you will save one million yen a year! And if you save one million a year, you can save thirty million by the time you retire at sixty if you are in your thirties now, or forty million if you are in your twenties. And if you invest it further at a compound interest rate of three per cent, you will have about 49 million and 77.6 million respectively, not including tax. You will have no more worries about retiring!'

A sound that was neither laughter nor sighing rose from the audience.

'I know what you're thinking. You think it's impossible, don't you? Admit it.'

Miho couldn't help but laugh and nod. From the corner of her eye, she noticed the guy next to her doing the same.

'You are now under my spell. Once you hear these numbers,

you will remember them always, no matter what. Before you know it, you will be thinking: *I'm going to save eighty thousand yen every month.* Even if that's impossible for you now, try and get as close to it as you can! Work to reach this goal! If you save eighty thousand a month, you can do whatever you like with the rest of your money! Spend your bonus however you want – apart from that twenty thousand yen, of course!'

At this, Ms Kurofune flung her arms wide, like an opera singer; there was a moment of silence as the audience gaped, then came a gale of laughter. But they were not laughing at her; this was a warm laugh of approval. Miho, too, giggled heartily, and her eyes naturally met those of the guy next to her, who gave a slight nod of acknowledgement.

'That three thousand yen you paid today is money well spent. Now, let's go through, step by step, how to save eighty thousand yen a month. The first thing is to review your fixed costs.'

Miho uttered an exclamation of surprise. Isn't that what Maho had said? After a good laugh at herself, she could no longer deny it: *You certainly do know what you're doing, Sis.* She didn't yet know if she would be able to do it too, but Miho meekly opened her notebook, and wrote down what the teacher said.

2

Looking for Work at the Age of Seventy-Three

Kotoko Mikuriya was in the midst of enjoying a fifteen-minute full-body massage in her state-of-the-art electric massage chair. While scanning the newspaper to the background accompaniment of its quiet whirring, she came across something that nearly made her jump out of her seat.

Mango Bank Retirement Bonus Campaign! Special Rate of 2% Annual Interest (before tax), she read.

Since her chair was reclined at an angle so low it was more like a bed than a seat, it was with some difficulty that she raised herself to a sitting position.

'Glasses, glasses,' she mumbled, eyes fixed on the newspaper as she scrabbled about with her hands, like the caricature of an old person in a comedy sketch. They were right beside her, on a table next to the chair. Settling them on her nose, she read through the fine print of the advertisement, slowly, and with great care.

'Let me see now . . . Mango Bank . . . retirement bonus campaign . . . special rate . . . two per cent annual interest. Only retirees and spouses over sixty eligible to apply. However—'

There was always a catch to these campaigns, which could be found in the fine print. Savvy consumer that Kotoko was, she naturally read this too. The minute lettering, no larger than a pinhead, was far, far smaller than anything else printed in the advertisement, and especially difficult for old eyes to glean, almost as if to say: *Don't bother trying, you won't like it!* Which is exactly why Kotoko had her glasses at the ready.

'Two per cent interest applies for the first three months on a minimum deposit of ten million yen, for a period of more than three months, after which the interest rate is 0.01 per cent . . . Yes, well, it would be, wouldn't it?'

That was how campaigns like this worked. They pulled in customers with eye-catching high interest rates that then dropped after a period of one to six months, to the usual level of fixed-term deposits. Still, 0.01% was better than in some banks. The current average interest rate on ordinary savings accounts at city banks was 0.001%.

'Ridiculous,' Kotoko was finally moved to comment. 'The bank must be making a killing at 0.001 per cent now that the economy's improved a bit.' But there was nothing to be gained by taking aim at the bank. 'Ten million yen for three months at two per cent, comes to . . . around fifty thousand yen in interest?'

Kotoko got out of her chair and went to the kitchen to extract a large well-worn abacus from a drawer, which she used to swiftly do the calculations. She had been a shop assistant in a Ginza department store after leaving high school, and was much faster with an abacus than a calculator.

'Bingo! Ten million yen for three months is ¥49,998 . . . subtract tax and it comes to ¥39,546. That's how much interest I could make.'

Kotoko picked up the smartphone she had been using for the last three years to do some research on Mango Bank.

'"Mango" as a name doesn't inspire much confidence, does it? But then nor does Tomato Bank. How *do* they come up with these silly names?'

Mango Bank, it turned out, was based in Miyazaki Prefecture, down in Kyushu, and until ten years ago had gone by the far more conventional name of Miyazaki Bank of Commerce and Industry.

Regional banks often ran such high-interest campaigns, with of course the aim of gaining access to the nest eggs of senior citizens. But it wasn't as if you had to actually present in person at these banks in far-flung cities; all you had to do was ring and ask for an information package to be posted, fill in the forms, open an account and deposit the money. A few years ago, there had been a rash of campaigns, with one bank even promising *5% interest guaranteed* and taking it upon themselves to offer, unasked for, projected models of how Kotoko's savings could be managed. The country had still been in a deep recession under the Democratic Party of Japan administration and it was an era of deflation: shares were cheap, the yen was high, and since there was nowhere else worth mentioning to park her money, Kotoko had briefly been tempted. Luckily, her granddaughter Maho, who used to work for a securities company, had stopped her when she was on the verge of being duped.

'Grandma, don't! I know it says they guarantee your money back plus five per cent, but it doesn't say anywhere how long they can take to do it. They could leave you waiting until you die. And if your principal is reduced in the meantime, they won't take responsibility – you'll only have yourself to blame. It's practically fraud!' Maho had been livid. 'It may be a big-name company, but they're ruthless.'

After that, however, the economy had undergone a bit of an upturn under the next administration's policy of Abenomics, so she might very well have earned that 5% after all. If she had, no doubt the people at the bank would have been preening and recommending further investments – with completely innocent expressions, of course. Ultimately, however, the system worked in the bank's favour.

Kotoko had been scared off from any further investing, until a friend had whispered in her ear about another way to make some pocket money and grow her savings. It wasn't investment exactly, rather clever use of the high-interest products that banks had begun developing to target senior citizens and their retirement bonuses. The idea was to find banks, like Mango, that were offering high interest rates for short periods, then shift the money from one bank to another.

When Kotoko asked Maho's advice, her granddaughter read through the material carefully before giving her assent.

'It should be okay,' she said, 'but I'm jealous, Gran. You never see banks offering this rate to young people. And we're the ones who could really do with higher interest rates to save for our futures!'

As much as Kotoko sympathised with her granddaughter, it wasn't enough to stop her from utilising whatever means were available to her. The banks were out to prey on senior citizens, which might not qualify as outright exploitation, but Kotoko felt compelled to match them in wiliness. Besides, it would be a great shame not to make good use of the hard-earned assets that her husband had left her, from his years of working at a trading company. He had died five years ago from lung cancer, despite only ever having smoked for a short period in his twenties. However, he'd almost never had regular health checks, and by the time he went to see the doctor about a terrible cough, the cancer was stage IV and already in his lymph glands.

Kotoko found it nerve-racking at first, having to shift a sum of ¥10 million. Once she got used to it, however, it was child's play. Whenever there was a bank within reasonable commuting distance, she would stuff the cash into a mountain-climbing rucksack and carry it there herself to deposit. In this fashion, she went around to all kinds of banks. It was no big deal to her to move the money once a month, or every three months. And though she had to fill in lots of forms, time was one thing she had no shortage of.

'Don't you worry what the bank staff think when you go switching money from place to place?' Maho teased her. Bank workers were generally accorded great respect in society, but

Kotoko became used to ignoring any qualms about what they might think.

Her goal had been to buy a massage chair entirely with the proceeds of the interest. And one year ago, after three years of saving, she finally achieved her goal. The chair she bought for more than ¥400,000 was the latest model, capable of giving her a thorough whole-body massage from the neck down to the tips of her toes, with no discomfort from overstimulation. Now her greatest pleasure in life was to lie in it every morning while she leisurely browsed through the newspaper from front to back.

Since last year, there had been a visible decline in gimmicky high-interest campaigns. Maybe the economy was on a downturn, or maybe more people were engaging in the same tactic as Kotoko. Whatever the reason, this advertisement for the Mango Bank campaign was the first big one Kotoko had seen in some time.

Here was a chance. And yet . . . She read through all the fine print, then abruptly put the newspaper down. *I already have my chair,* she thought. *There's nothing I can think of that I want now. Admittedly, not wanting for anything is a luxury in itself, and I am grateful for that, but still . . .*

There had been a time when she was always wanting one thing or another. When her sons were small, they used to adore the tiny plastic bottles of Yakult probiotic drink that were new on the market back then. Nowadays these were low-cost items available in supermarkets, like many other products, but back then they were so expensive that Kotoko couldn't afford them. The pleasure they brought to her sons' faces was too much to resist, and besides, she had heard that

Yakult was good for the health, so she had gone without meals herself to buy them.

The family had not been poor, not by any means. They lived comfortably, and everybody else around them was in more or less the same financial situation. But there was no money to waste in those days.

Kotoko's thoughts returned with a jolt to the present. If she was to make anything from this campaign, she would have to phone the bank to request the documentation, fill in the forms and return them. Then she would need to go to the bank where her money was currently held and fill in more forms to withdraw a huge lump sum of cash. For the first time ever, it felt like too much bother. *Strange,* she thought, *when all I have to do is move a bit of money around to net nearly forty thousand yen in interest.*

Doing this used to give Kotoko a thrill, and she enjoyed managing and keeping track of her accounts. It was like a game, almost. But now she had her chair, Kotoko realised that without any concrete purpose, there was little fun in simply moving money around. It was merely hard work.

However, this was not the only reason that Kotoko could not rouse herself to shift the ¥10 million. Something else had arisen, unexpectedly.

When her husband died, she had been left with his retirement bonus plus a post office savings account with several million yen. The pension they had lived on until then, however, was halved upon his death, and Kotoko was forced to dip into the post office account from time to time. Now, there were only a few hundred thousand yen left in it.

This was exactly the right time to boost her savings. But if she did, she would not be able to access her money again for three months, and if she had any kind of unforeseen expense in the meantime, she would be in trouble.

Once upon a time, several hundred thousand yen had seemed like an inordinately huge sum to Kotoko, and she couldn't believe how quickly it had dwindled. The ¥10 million lump sum consequently became even more precious as a source of reassurance, a safety net in case she had to go into a nursing facility, or renovate her own place for home care. The thought of having to break into the account filled her with anxiety. Ever since last year when she first started thinking about it, this worry had been constantly at the back of her mind. She had fretted and fretted, but, with no solution in sight, decided not to dwell on it any more. Seeing the campaign advertisement from Mango Bank, however, had thrust it back to the forefront of her thoughts.

'I wouldn't mind your problem,' Yasuo Komori said, chuckling heartily after hearing from Kotoko about the retirement bonus campaign – minus the part about her pension not being enough to live off.

'I'm not so sure you would.'

'If I had the chance to make forty thousand yen, I'd do it in a flash. I can easily live off one million yen a year, so forty thousand would be two weeks' living expenses. I could travel for a month on that. Bangkok's nice this time of year, though Khaosan isn't cheap any more. Or I could go to Malaysia – chill out in Malacca or somewhere round there. Then again, hanging out at home and reading isn't so bad either.' Yasuo's suntanned face broadened into a smile.

Though much younger than Kotoko, the two had become friends after a chance encounter last November at a large homeware store. Kotoko had been inspecting a big case of viola seedlings, on sale at ¥600 for the lot. The store had obviously overstocked and been unable to sell them all, so now the plants were way past their best and had been put out for almost nothing. There were thirty seedlings in the case, which worked out at ¥20 a plant – an incredible bargain. She squatted down, carefully examining each seedling. Some had no flowers, some were brown and wilted with the flowers just hanging on, while others were still in full bloom and had long stems, but were past their prime.

As anyone with the right kind of horticultural experience would know, violas can be revived. Replanted in good soil with a decent dash of fertiliser and the long stems and wilted flowers pruned back, they will soon start blooming again. It was still November. Kotoko was willing to bet that with the right treatment, these seedlings could keep blooming until early May.

Thirty plants, however, was a rather a lot. Kotoko did not live in the neighbourhood and would have to transport them home on her electric bicycle, which was one problem, but an even greater issue was that she did not have enough space in her garden. If only there were fifteen, she could plant them by the front door and have them blooming in an eye-catching display in less than a month. For a mere ¥300 . . .

Most of all, she was reluctant to leave them because she

knew that if she didn't buy the seedlings, there was a good chance they would remain unsold and be thrown away. The thought was simply too sad and upsetting. It was at that moment she heard a young male voice say, 'How about that! What a great price!'

Looking over her shoulder, Kotoko saw a tanned young man with a sunny smile standing behind her, and looking down at her as she squatted. Hurriedly she rose to her feet.

'That's a great price,' he said. 'I'd take them home but I can't use this many.'

'Exactly,' Kotoko responded impulsively. Ordinarily, she was wary of strangers. An elderly woman living alone, with what could reasonably be called some degree of wealth – who knew when one might be conned by a stranger? She had heard plenty of horror stories on TV, and read about them in the newspapers and weekly magazines that she occasionally perused at the library. But today she was in the gardening section, where her joy at encountering someone else who shared her opinion led her to let down her guard. And this young man, while not handsome, had a likeable but slightly goofy smile that disarmed her caution. 'I just know I could bring them back to health,' she said.

The young man crouched down and gently caressed the seedlings. 'There doesn't seem to be any problem with their roots.'

Kotoko didn't know him from a bar of soap, but she was happy at the opportunity to simply talk gardening. 'If they were replanted and topped, they'd pick up in no time,' she said.

'I bet they would,' he replied. 'I don't have space for them all in my garden. I already planted most of them a month ago when the price of these was still eighty yen a seedling. I've still got a bit of room, but not enough for thirty.'

'Eighty yen's not a bad price. I couldn't hold out, and bought them when the price dropped from one fifty, to one hundred.'

'Ah, you jumped the gun.'

'I just wanted to get them in early so I could enjoy them at the beginning of autumn.'

'I know how you feel,' he said. 'I would've bought then too, if I'd had the money.' Gently, he touched a browned flower. 'Do you think they'll be thrown out if nobody buys them?'

'Do you want to go halves?' It was hard to say whose mouth the words popped out from first. They looked at each other and laughed.

'Yes, let's share.'

Kotoko tried to pay slightly more than half, but Yasuo flatly refused to let her. She knew, from the little they had said to each other, that he didn't appear to be well off. But his willingness to split the bill fairly made a good impression and convinced her that he was not underhand with money. While they were paying for the seedlings and divvying them up, Yasuo told Kotoko that he lived in an old, small house with a garden, located on the other side of the Jujo main shopping street from Kotoko's house. He offered to deliver Kotoko's share of the plants to her house on his motorcycle, but she declined as she still knew nothing about him. Perhaps he was married with small children, and that's why he had no money, she mused, or maybe he was a shift-worker like Maho's husband, and was offduty now.

After that day, Kotoko occasionally ran into Yasuo at the same homeware store where they had first met, and in the Jujo main street. It was strange how their paths kept crossing. Whenever Yasuo spotted Kotoko, he would approach her with a big smile, as if he had found an old acquaintance or lover, and make friendly remarks such as, 'How're the violas doing? Mine are in full bloom,' or 'It's getting cold now,' or 'Do you think it's a good idea to cut the violas back once more before the end of the year?'

When spring came, he asked Kotoko to have tea with him. She was still wary enough to think that this might be a ploy to get her to join some kind of weird religion, but thought, *Well, if he does, I can just say no,* and accompanied him to an inexpensive coffee shop. There she learned that not only did he not have children, he was not even married, nor had a regular job, and that he spent half the year away from home either travelling abroad or working in other parts of the country for long periods. Apparently, the fifty-year-old house he lived in had been his grandmother's, and since no one was living there now, he was provisionally taking care of it.

She also learned that he was a serious 'grandma's boy'.

'I might not have any money, but Grandma took good care of her garden, so I want to at least keep it tidy for her,' he told Kotoko, earning her instant approval.

*

'You did well to save up enough money,' Kotoko told Yasuo when he came by to leave his house key with her. He was about to go overseas, and in his absence Kotoko had promised to water the garden and air the house for him, taking over from an elderly neighbour who used to do this, but had gone to live with her daughter in Yokohama after her health began to falter.

'Granny, how can you let a man like that into the house?' Maho had demanded sharply when Kotoko confided in her about Yasuo. 'He could be a thief, or mugger!'

'But I'm the one with the master key to his house.'

'That might be a trick just to lull you.'

'Oh, I don't know.'

'He doesn't even have a proper job.'

It was true, Yasuo did not have regular employment. But ever since she had begun talking with him, Kotoko had come to think that it was precisely because he did not have a regular job that his character and diligence could not be called into question. Much of his part-time work seemed to consist of seasonal jobs in Okinawa and Hokkaido, and it sounded as if Yasuo had the knack of being able to quickly fit in anywhere and learn the ropes. He was mindful of his elders and listened attentively to everybody, qualities that enabled him to live the way he did, like a migratory bird.

Besides, once she started going to Yasuo's house, Kotoko had met other people in the neighbourhood, and in talking with them had learned that his background and current situation were exactly as he himself had described. The upshot of all this was that not only did Kotoko now trust Yasuo, she was also quite fond of him.

'I'll bring you back a present. Don't forget the green peas and snap peas are almost ready to be harvested, so please help yourself to them.'

The plants required little watering at this time of year, once a week being quite sufficient for those that grew in the ground, but even if more frequent watering were necessary, Kotoko was a pensioner who had plenty of time on her hands so it would not have been a problem for her.

'I will do that then. Thank you very much,' she said. 'I'm much obliged.' It was then that Kotoko had let slip about her quandary over the Mango Bank campaign.

'I can only dream about that kind of money,' he said.

For a moment Kotoko regretted revealing how much she had in savings. Yasuo gave an easy, big-hearted smile, seemingly unaware of her suspicions.

'It's not so much. Everyone my age has money, you know.'

'I suppose so. After my grandmother died, we discovered old ten-thousand- and hundred-yen notes on the family altar, some that aren't even in circulation any more. I think Grandma was hoping they'd become valuable. It was about the only thing she had in terms of estate.'

'What about the house?'

'An old house like that is only worth what you'd get for it as firewood.'

'Don't talk like that. The house is on land in Jujo, right? It might not be as valuable as it was during the bubble, but that land would still be worth a nice price.'

'You're right, I suppose. Are you one of those thrifty people who saved and economised to get where you are now, Kotoko?'

Kotoko shook her head. 'I'm telling you – I did nothing out of the ordinary. Times were good.' She didn't really want to talk about her own money. But Yasuo persisted, oblivious.

'Are you talking about the post-war period of high growth, and the bubble era?'

'That's part of it. When I started working, the entry-level wage was about ten thousand yen. By the time I quit it was fifty times that. Solid growth in the economy is the reason we were able to get to where we are now,' Kotoko couldn't help adding, even though she wanted to drop the subject. It's not as if it was a topic she disliked talking about, and she naturally had opinions about what she read in the newspaper or saw on TV. 'I feel sorry for young people today, who don't get the benefits from that period,' she muttered in a low voice to herself. 'But I've always used a *kakeibo* to track household accounts, like my mother taught me. That's about the sum of it.'

'Kakeibo?' Yasuo squawked. 'That is the farthest thing from my life.'

'My mother was born in 1924. Kakeibo was first mentioned in a women's magazine in 1904, the year of the Russo-Japanese War,' Kotoko said. She was sure that being young he had no interest in hearing about things like that, but at least he made a show of listening to her, and making the right noises when appropriate. *Maybe he's just naturally good-natured,* she thought.

Even after talking with Yasuo, Kotoko still could not make up her mind what to do about the Mango Bank campaign. If she was going to sign up, it was best to do it sooner rather than later, as first she would have to call the bank and ask for the materials to be sent, and then she would need to get moving with the procedures to withdraw her money from the bank where it was currently deposited … In spite of the fact that this was all Kotoko could think about, her body would not move into action.

I don't understand, she thought. *There was a time when I would gladly have thrown myself into doing all the required work. Now I just lie about in my massage chair. And today I'm in a dream too. It's true, as Yasuo suggested, that I could use the interest for living expenses, but if I did there's no escaping the reality that my pension is not enough and I'm strapped for cash.*

Kotoko heaved a loud sigh. The kind that is so loud even the person doing it notices and thinks, *Oh, now I'm sighing.* She roused herself to get out of the chair. *Time to do my kakeibo and have a good think.*

Kotoko's husband had retired from his job in a trading company at the age of sixty, then worked as an executive of a subsidiary company until sixty-five. When the couple began their lives on the pension, they had received just under ¥260,000 once every two months. Although it was not a large sum, they still had plenty of money in their postal savings account, and often travelled. There was never a time when they felt an acute shortage of money.

When Kotoko became a widow, however, her pension was reduced to around ¥80,000 a month. This hadn't fazed her at first. *I won't have many expenses, if I just live modestly without extravagances and take good care of the house it'll be all right.* But things didn't work out that way. For one thing, cooking for one person is not a great deal less expensive than cooking for two. Also, once she was on her own, Kotoko experienced a dramatic increase in her social life: casual invitations from old friends to lunch at a new Italian restaurant and so forth, or to go for a trip to Fukushima to eat peaches. While her husband was still alive these had not been such a common occurrence, but now she received an invitation practically every month. If she accepted, then there was the question of what clothes and shoes to wear – after all she couldn't always wear the same thing.

She could always say no of course, but the older Kotoko got, the more she valued time spent with friends and family. She saw it as the most important thing in her remaining years. Her friends were also all unanimous in saying that there was no point in taking money with them to the afterlife or the grave.

Kotoko's problem was that she did not know how much money she would need in future for things like nursing care and other health expenses if she became ill.

Spend! Because you can't take it with you.

Economise! Because you can never know how much money you will need.

You can be sure that anyone wrestling with these two conflicting voices in their head is elderly.

Only recently had one of Kotoko's friends told her, 'The cost of nursing care is nine hundred thousand yen a year on average, so if you need nursing for five years it will cost you over five million yen.'

Hearing this had only strengthened Kotoko's reluctance to touch the ten million yen. *If only the gods could tell me what to do,* she thought, opening up her kakeibo. Wouldn't it be great to be told: *Your life expectancy will be eighty years and you will die of cancer, so there is no need to provide for nursing care.* Or, *You will not have any major illness but will die in your sleep in the early hours of the morning at the age of seventy-eight.* Or, *You will become bedridden after a fall, so you should save up.*

The shock of knowing would be enough to make you cry, but surely it would be some relief to know what the future held? In the absence of any such considerate god, however, the only method that Kotoko knew of for finding temporary peace of mind was to keep tab of her accounts in her kakeibo.

She had been very anxious when she and her husband had first embarked on life on the pension, but going to the bookshop and finding special editions of kakeibo books such as *Kakeibo for Senior Citizens* and *Pensioners' Kakeibo* had helped alleviate her worries.

The kakeibo for pensioners was different from previous kakeibo she had used in that each month's page started on the 15th – pension day. There was also a full column dedicated to medical expenses, and allowance had been made for two months' worth of calculations to be combined into one. *Kakeibo for Senior Citizens* was modelled on the first kakeibo household budgeting book created in Japan by journalist Motoko Hani, and Kotoko felt reassured by the familiar cover that reminded her of Madam Hani. After comparing various styles, Kotoko chose *Kakeibo for Senior Citizens* to use for her first year of life on the pension, and then switched to a simpler and cheaper version from then on.

Opening up her kakeibo, she took the receipts from

yesterday's supermarket shopping from her purse, and industriously set about carefully entering all the figures. Already she felt calmer.

About a week after Yasuo had left for overseas, Kotoko received a phone call from her daughter-in-law, Tomoko. Tomoko always called from the landline at home, and used a cell phone rather than a smartphone. Apparently, she had no intention of changing over. Her daughters, Maho and Miho, often grumbled about this. 'Mum is so behind the times. If she had a smartphone, at least we could use LINE to keep in contact. It's like the landline exists for her.' Tomoko was in her fifties, an age group that was often surprisingly more conservative than Kotoko's.

Tomoko's generation had missed out on computer training in the workplace, and she had always struggled with devices and the internet as a result. It was one reason why her daughters, who were so proficient in these, were always having to help their mother with things. Even now, when Tomoko didn't understand something, she would it look up in a dictionary or go to the library to search for a book. If she still couldn't find the answer, she would call her daughters and have them look it up on the internet for her.

When Tomoko said, 'Actually, I have a favour to ask, Mother,' Kotoko braced herself. *Surely, she's not going to ask* me *to look it up on the internet, too?*

'It's about the osechi dishes we ate at New Year.'

Kotoko was not expecting this. 'Osechi? What's that got to do with anything?'

'Do you remember that I learn English?'

Kotoko did. The thing about Tomoko that impressed Kotoko most, was her enthusiasm for study and desire to improve. As was typical of many women whose twenties had been during the bubble era, Tomoko was always dabbling in activities such as yoga, tennis, flower-arranging and the like. She had majored in French literature at university and had continued to study English and French ever since. Even while the girls were undergoing their tertiary and secondary education – with school fees no small expense – Tomoko had attended inexpensive classes at the Ward Community Centre. Kotoko had heard that Tomoko's dream was to go on a luxury cruise once her husband, Kazuhiko, retired, and speak English and French with people from other countries.

It rankled with Kotoko that not once had Tomoko ever asked her to join them. Not that she had a burning desire to go on a cruise, but she did sometimes think it would be nice if Tomoko invited her somewhere once at least, even if just as a courtesy. She would not have thought anything of the sort about her grandchildren, but when it came to her daughter-in-law, Kotoko could never help being dissatisfied. Though Kotoko had always been conscious of trying to extend a helping hand, Tomoko simply parried any offer with a smile, and if Kotoko tried to get closer, she would feel as if she were being brushed off. Despite having known each other for many years, deep down, Kotoko had the sense that Tomoko never let down her guard with her.

'Ah, yes, it's wonderful you've kept it up all these years,'

Kotoko concurred. Naturally she would not let any sign of her discontent show.

'Our teacher, Elaine, is lovely. The classes are a lot of fun.'

'Well, that's the best thing, isn't it?' agreed Kotoko.

'The other day we were talking about how each of us had spent the New Year holiday, and showed pictures of our families. I showed a photo of the osechi dishes we ate. Everybody complimented me on how beautiful they looked, and the next thing I knew they asked me to teach them how to make osechi.'

Kotoko couldn't help laughing. 'Are you sure they weren't just being polite?'

'I thought so too at first, but it seems they're actually serious.'

'I can't imagine a foreigner eating osechi.'

'No, no, you've got it wrong. It wasn't the teacher, but the other students who asked. They said they want to learn from me.'

'Are they young people? Or recently married?'

If they were, then Kotoko could understand. Nevertheless, she couldn't help feeling that making osechi was something that should be learned at home, as each family had their own way of doing things.

'No, not all,' Tomoko replied. 'Some are young, but there are others my age or older.'

As Tomoko explained it, apparently there were women who, after marriage, had always spent New Year at their in-laws', naturally enough, but if the husband's family were in the habit of buying osechi dishes instead of making them, then they never had the opportunity to learn for themselves. Then, when the mother-in-law passed away and they went to cook them, they didn't know where to start.

'But making osechi is nothing special,' Kotoko objected. 'And there are any number of cookbooks and end-of-year special features in magazines. Why don't they just read those?'

'I agree. But sometimes, it can be surprisingly hard to start doing something new at this age.'

'I see.'

'Anyway, because it would be difficult to make everything in one day, there was talk of them coming here once a month. We would make a few dishes each time and then chat over tea. I wondered if you would mind helping – I mean, you were the one who taught me how to make candied dried sardines and two-coloured egg, weren't you? And I think it would much better for them to learn properly from someone more expert than I am.'

'Oh, but I couldn't, I have no idea how to teach.'

Even as she spoke, however, Kotoko was not unhappy about the idea; in fact she was delighted. Any negative thoughts she had had about Tomoko evaporated, to be replaced by an appreciation of her daughter-in-law's gentle charm. She agreed to the proposal and to hold the first osechi cooking class the following month. The two women animatedly discussed what to make in the first lesson, eventually plumping for old standards such as chestnut *kinton*, simmered chicken with vegetables and candied dried sardines.

*

The Osechi Cooking Class was a great success. Kotoko was surprised at Tomoko's charging ¥5,000 per person to cover tea and ingredients, but six people quickly signed up and there were others who said they wanted to join in next time. One person brought an American woman with them, adding a glamorous touch of international exchange to the gathering, and people snapped numerous photos with their smartphones to upload to social media.

Tomoko had prepared a written list of ingredients and instructions in advance, which she handed out, and explained the process as they set to work. Kotoko was appreciative of Tomoko's know-how, gleaned from her wealth of experience in different classes, as to how best to conduct the lesson. Once the cooking was done, they all sat down to taste the finished dishes and chat over tea and snacks.

'Thank you so much, Mother,' Tomoko said with a bow to Kotoko once everybody had left.

'It was nothing. I enjoyed myself.'

This was no lie; the class had been a reminder of how much she liked meeting people. Kotoko had been happy at the way everyone was so supportive and respectful of her, since she was the oldest present, and asked her many questions. Before she knew it, she had overcome her initial diffidence about knowing anything worth teaching, and found herself chatting away about topics such as child-rearing and old age.

As Kotoko was leaving, Tomoko handed her an envelope with 'honorarium' written on it. Kotoko refused several times, as was polite, saying 'I couldn't possibly,' until Tomoko stuffed it into her handbag.

'These things must be done properly,' she said. 'If you don't accept it, I can't ask you again.' Then she added with a mischievous smile that she had also taken her own cut.

When Kotoko checked the contents of the envelope after arriving home, she found a ¥5,000 note inside.

Kotoko was awoken by the bang and clatter of the newspaper being delivered to the box outside her front door. The small room next to it, where Kotoko had been sleeping, had once been the children's room, and she was always awoken by the newspaper delivery when she slept there. At four in the morning, it was still dark and cold. She put on the fleece gown next to her bed and went out into the hallway. The gown had been a present from her granddaughters to replace her *tanzen* padded kimono, which they said was too heavy and not warm enough. The fleece was indeed so soft and convenient that she never wore the tanzen again.

After collecting the newspaper, she took it down to the kitchen-dining room, turned the coffee maker on and opened up the paper. Recently, she had taken to quickly scanning the headlines before turning her attention to the advertising flyer inserts that came with the newspaper. The ¥5,000 that Kotoko had received from Tomoko had had a big impact on her: it made her happy. Simply happy. Happy that she, too, was still capable of earning money. When she had pulled the note out from the envelope after arriving home that day, her heart filled with an indescribable joy, a satisfaction such as she had not experienced in years. She was proud to have something other than 'pension' to enter into the income column of her kakeibo for the first time in a very long while. Kotoko herself was puzzled at the extremity of her emotion – worried, even, that she might be having heart palpitations. *Was it, at bottom, that I just wanted money?* she thought to herself in bed. *Is that all?* She was saddened by her own shallowness at first, but then revised her opinion: *No, that's not all it is, maybe I simply want to be appreciated.* This felt closer to the truth, but still didn't explain everything; after all Maho was appreciative whenever she looked after Saho, and Yasuo too, for her watering his garden. *Which means,* she concluded, *I want to be appreciated* and *paid.*

I want to work. The thought popped into her head. *I want to work?* She was stunned by the realisation. At seventy-three years old – an age when there was every chance of keeling over at any time and even her grandchildren teased her about going batty – she wanted to go out to work again.

Impossible, she thought, shaking her head.

Of course she'd seen discussions on TV about the government's plan for promoting a 'Society with the Dynamic Engagement of All Citizens', but surely it was not feasible for someone over seventy to work? *If only I was in my sixties, at least,* she thought. Kotoko dwelled on this until sleep overtook her.

Then, the very next day – just like that – she came across a job advert on a leaflet inserted into the newspaper: *Daily cleaning of flats | No age limit | No experience required | Senior citizens welcome | We await your application!* Kotoko carefully set it aside.

Up to now, she had only ever considered covering her living

costs from her savings and pension, but perhaps she could continue to earn money? This hope spurred her into action, and since then, she eagerly searched the newspaper flyers every morning. One day she found one from a company recruiting housekeeping staff to dispatch. The phrase ' jumped out at her. On another occasion she was in a convenience store in the Jujo shopping district, when she heard an in-store announcement about a part-time job opening: 'We are seeking people to work with us. Housewives, first-timers, the elderly and people from overseas are all welcome. You, too, are welcome – won't you work with us?'

The announcement had stopped Kotoko in her tracks. She thought of the labour shortage, and the government plan for a Society with the Dynamic Engagement of All Citizens … Maybe this announcement was for real. She recalled it as she searched the newspaper in the early morning. Her ambition to find work, something she was too embarrassed to even say out loud, might not be too much to hope for after all.

'Ahem, seventy-three, did you say?' said the convenience-store manager, who had introduced himself as Saito, scrutinising Kotoko's CV with a quizzical expression. He looked about the same age as Yasuo. A chill swept through her. She flushed and wanted to disappear from the spot.

Kotoko was at the convenience store where she had heard the in-store announcement proclaiming 'senior citizens wanted!' and boldly gone up to the cash register to enquire.

'Um, excuse me, about this part-time job advertisement … I wonder if I could apply?'

'Of course! Please bring your CV in!' she had been told by the young man who was now standing in front her.

In spite of which, he was telling her, 'I am sorry, Mrs Mikuriya, you looked so young. Not at all in your seventies. I would have guessed late fifties or sixties.'

Kotoko couldn't tell if this was mere flattery, or he was serious, but she was not pleased to hear that in this moment.

'I never dreamed you were in your seventies. And you have a terrific CV.'

'But I'm no good?' Kotoko wished she could shrink though the floor. *What was an old lady like me thinking of, applying for a job in a place like this?*

'I'm not saying no,' protested Saito, flapping both hands at her ambiguously.

'Head office doesn't have any specific regulation, either. But . . . you know. The reality is that the people in their seventies we've had working here before, found it very hard and ended up quitting, most inconveniently. It wasn't just the cash register they couldn't get used to, but various other terminals and machines they were required to operate. Maybe if you were in your sixties . . .' Kotoko heard him add in a low voice, as she beat a hasty retreat from the store.

I want to work. Kotoko thought about how she could make this small dream come true. Well, maybe small wasn't the right word for it, maybe grand was a better way to put it for a person in their seventies.

After her rejection at the convenience store, Kotoko emailed Yasuo for his advice. Asking a relative stranger like him was much easier than talking to her own family. Though the content of her email verged more on complaint than consultation, she felt confident he would not dismiss her outright.

Sure enough, she received a reply immediately:

> Restaurant staff, housekeeper, after-school care assistant, security guard staff, building superintendent, nursing-care provider, cleaner, hospital-meal preparation, school-lunch preparation, gardener, car-park staff, day-care assistant, cook's assistant etc., etc. That's just a list of vacancies I found for over 65s after a quick search on the internet. Tokyo Metropolitan Government also has a vocational support centre for seniors, and their career counselling is supposed to be good. Why not try it? Good luck. I'm cheering for you!

Kotoko was grateful beyond words. That after reading her email, in a foreign country, he had promptly done this for her. She was touched especially by the last line. If Yasuo says so, I have to do my best for him, too. She had been almost ready to give up after the fiasco at the convenience store, but now Kotoko's determination was reignited.

'First thing you need to do is to sort out in your mind why and how you want to work,' the counsellor at the career-counselling session for seniors began. 'If you're not clear on that you could end up searching indiscriminately, and potentially not finding anything at all, or taking whatever comes along and then resigning straight away.'

'Oh.'

Kotoko had gone to the Hello Work government employment centre with the intention of making an appointment for counselling, but upon being told that no appointment was necessary and she could request one on the spot, she had done just that. Thirty minutes later her interview with a woman in her forties commenced.

'Do you have your CV?'

'No, I didn't bring it as I didn't think I could have counselling today.'

Without a murmur, the woman asked Kotoko about her history and entered it into the computer.

'Before marriage you worked at a department store in Ginza. Is that the extent of your work experience?'

'Ah, yes.'

This counsellor came across as a nice-enough person, and not at all intimidating. Nevertheless, Kotoko felt as if she had been told that her career amounted to nothing much. Her eyes fell to the ground. She had been in charge of the ground-floor scarf and handkerchief section, with a sales record par excellence. The department store was also where she had met her husband, who was working in an office nearby, and came in every day to buy a new handkerchief from her. Once he had bought every available kind of men's handkerchief, he declared himself. But there was no point in mentioning that here.

'Do you have any hobbies or special skills? Some people utilise these when seeking work.'

Kotoko's hobby was buying discount flower seedlings. She could bring even the most wilted of flowers back to life, but there wouldn't be any call for that, would there? she thought. *And I can calculate interest rates, but that's all I know about economics. Of course I've always done my accounts using a kakeibo, but none of that counts as a 'career' or 'skill', does it?* 'Er ... nothing worth mentioning,' Kotoko replied. 'No, there's nothing,' she added, her voice growing quieter.

'But you raised children and did the housework, didn't you? That's a major career.'

At last, Kotoko could lift her eyes and smile. 'Thank you. Don't you think it's strange for an old lady like me to want to work?'

'Not in the least. There are many others like you. But it might be a good idea to sort out your thoughts first.'

The counsellor went on to give examples of reasons for wanting to work: 'to be of use to other people and society', 'to make use of skills', 'to make use of hobbies', 'to support someone', 'to be more involved in society', 'for self-improvement', 'to earn an income' and so on.

'There are many more. And of course, you may have a combination of reasons. But I think it might be a good idea for you to give the question some more thought, Ms Mikuriya, before you start looking for a position.'

On her way home, Kotoko went over what the Hello Work counsellor had told her. Why had she been unable to simply say to the woman that she wanted money? It was a shock to realise how proud she was. It wasn't that she wanted full-time employment with all the perks, but how much easier life would be if she could only earn ¥30,000–40,000 a month.

Well, it's good I can admit that, she thought. *If I had that much extra income every month, I wouldn't have to dip into my savings, or hesitate every time I wanted to spend money on hobbies like travelling and gardening. Not that my gardening costs amount to much anyway, since all I do is buy plants put out for clearance. But there is also a part of me that would like to be of help to young people, if possible. And it would be nice to meet new people. If I work hard and save some money, then I can also leave something for my grandchildren.*

What type of job should I try for? Housekeeper? Or 'home services' as it's called these days. I don't dislike housework, but I don't like it enough to make it my job, nor am I particularly good at it. Besides, now that I'm finally done with looking after a family, I don't really feel like doing all that again at this age.

There's nursing care and cleaning, but I don't have a particular yearning to work in those fields. No, when it comes down to it, I'd like to work in sales again. I'm used to it, and I like talking to customers. Would that be too much to hope for?

'This might sound odd coming from someone in my position, but many senior citizens find jobs through introductions from acquaintances. What about letting people know that you are looking for work, and asking for their advice?' the Hello Work counsellor had said at the end of their session.

'Hmm. I don't think any of my friends or family could introduce me to a job.' The only person she had talked to was Yasuo, and Kotoko didn't think he would know of any jobs suitable for her. Especially with his own situation being so fluid.

'Don't be so hasty to jump to conclusions. Job offers sometimes come from the most unexpected places. The best outcomes are usually when someone receives an introduction through somebody they know, not through sending a CV.'

Kotoko sighed deeply. *I bet that was just a nice way of getting rid of me,* she thought.

The following week, Maho came over for a visit. This came about after an exchange Kotoko had with Maho on the LINE messaging app they used to keep in touch.

Yesterday I had an email from Yasuo, she had written casually to Maho.

Grandma, are you still seeing that man! came Maho's angry reply.

He's not that kind of man. He's a good person.

He'll steal the hair from your bottom if you keep talking like that.

That's a vulgar thing to say. (laugh)

It's no laughing matter.

After a while, another message arrived. *Coming over tomorrow! I have to check you're not being conned!* This was accompanied by an 'angry' face stamp.

Kotoko shrugged. Despite her protestations, Maho was the one she should be more worried about stealing the hair from her bottom. Whenever Maho came to visit she would eat lunch, of course, and an early dinner, and then take food wrapped up for her husband to eat on top of that. She never missed any stock of food Kotoko might have cooked up and left in the fridge, and she also took home fruit and vegetables, as well as any packages of mid- or end-of-year food gifts lying around. And not only food; Maho's eyes would light on recent purchases of items such as towels, sheets and mats, and she would plead, 'Grandma, this is so cute, can I have it?' Once she had even reached for cotton underpants that Kotoko had bought in bulk, but Kotoko snatched them back. 'Leave those alone, you're not old enough for them yet.'

Kotoko would laugh with Tomoko, who was also frequently subjected to such visits from Maho and Saho, that it was like being ransacked by a gang of kids. Kotoko, however, was not as upset as her words might suggest – although that could change if her savings ran short in future. She had time on her hands and enjoyed spending it with her granddaughter and sweet little great-granddaughter. In fact, she was thankful, even, for these visits. Maho understood this, which was why she felt free to conduct her raids. Kotoko wanted to earn money for her grandchildren's sake too.

Next afternoon, Maho showed up with Saho and, with hardly a word of greeting, immediately demanded, 'Grandma, what on earth did you tell that man?'

Resigning herself to being reprimanded, Kotoko related to Maho all that she had told Yasuo about her savings, her mother's kakeibo and her desire to work.

'If you told him about the interest, he'd be able to work out how much savings you have,' said Maho, zooming in on the interest, just as Kotoko thought she would. 'Do you have ten million yen saved up, Grandma?' she said, driving home the point, then laughed.

As could only be expected of a former securities employee, Maho had made quick mental calculations simply from hearing ¥40,000 for three months at 2% interest.

'It's not as if I told him where my bank book and personal seal are,' Kotoko protested.

'I should think not. If you'd told him that you would have had to move immediately!'

'He's not a bad person. I'll introduce you.'

'I have no interest in meeting him, but for your sake I will. Okay? Taiyo can come too, so he can see that you have people watching out for you.'

Putting aside the part about watching out for her, Kotoko thought it was not a bad thing for these young people who lived in the same area to meet. 'Yes, why not? I'll let you know when he comes back from overseas.'

'The way you talk makes him sound like a boyfriend,' Maho said, looking fierce. 'So, what was it you said about the kakeibo?' she asked.

'Oh, that's right, I've never told you much about my grandmother and mother, have I?'

'I've never heard anything.'

That's right, thought Kotoko. She'd mentioned them in the past to Tomoko, who seemed somewhat irritated and bored, therefore Kotoko had never raised the topic again. But on reflection, a grandchild was not the same as a daughter-in-law. A granddaughter might be more interested since it concerned her direct family history.

'My grandmother and mother both kept a kakeibo during the war,' Kotoko began. Then with a warning that it might take some time, she launched into her story.

The history of kakeibo begins with the release of the first volume in 1904 by Fujin no Tomo, publisher of *The Women's*

Friend magazine, under the supervision of editor-in-chief Motoko Hani. Madam Hani also wrote an advice column in the magazine called *Questions and Answers about Household Management*, in which she addressed readers' queries about budgeting.

Kotoko's own mother, Mine Ushio, had been born in 1924, and Kotoko herself came into the world about twenty years later, which meant that she was one or two generations younger than the first generation of kakeibo users. Kotoko's grandmother and mother were both regular readers of another rival magazine called *The Housewife's Friend*. Mine apparently said that her mother preferred this over *The Women's Friend* because it presented a more modern, down-to-earth image of housewives, and also because Motoko Hani was 'a tad strict'. Therefore, when Shufu no Tomo, publisher of *The Housewife's Friend*, released their first edition of *A Model Kakeibo* in 1930, she rushed to buy it, and was proud of using it faithfully until the day she died.

When Mine later married and started a family, naturally she also used a kakeibo published by Shufu no Tomo to keep her household accounts. Shufu no Tomo continued to publish a kakeibo during and after the war, changing its name to *The Daily Life Kakeibo*.

Kotoko explained this all roughly to Maho, assuming that it would not interest her greatly since it was all old stories from the past, but Maho listened attentively.

'I get it! It wasn't so long ago there was a rush of magazines about economising with titles like *Thank you!*, *The Good Wife* and *Good Morning Housewives*. Mum used to buy *The Good*

Wife sometimes, but I liked *Thank you!* better because it was more stylish. *The Good Wife* and *Good Morning Housewives* eventually went out of print.'

'*A Notebook for Everyday Life* was another influential women's magazine launched after the war,' Kotoko continued, 'and there was fierce competition for sales between this, *The Housewife's Friend* and *The Women's Friend*.'

Much as she enjoyed talking about women's magazines, Kotoko steered conversation back to its main topic – kakeibo. 'My mother was a great user of Shufu no Tomo's kakeibo, but the really impressive thing about it was the fact that the company managed to keep publishing it all throughout the war,' Kotoko said heatedly.

Maho listened and merely nodded as she stroked the sleeping Saho's back.

Kotoko felt a little sad. Young people probably had no idea what an achievement that was. 'It was a very difficult thing to do, you know. I have no memories of the time, since I was born during the war, but it was quite a feat to keep publishing at a time when there were severe shortages of everything. It just goes to show how much kakeibo were valued.'

'I do have some idea, you know – we learned about the war at school, and I've seen stuff on TV,' Maho said with a forced smile, surprised by Kotoko's intensity.

'Apart from in 1943 and 1945, kakeibo have been in continual publication. When the war ended in 1945, Japan experienced a period of tremendous inflation, when the price of things went up like mad.'

'The opposite of the deflation we had not so long ago.'

'Something that cost fifty yen one day, would be a hundred yen a few days later. Things couldn't be bought with money, you had to barter with kimonos or buy them on the black market. But even under those conditions people continued to keep detailed records in their kakeibo.'

'That can't have been easy when the value of money was so crazy.'

'In the last year of the war my mother kept a handmade kakeibo. I saw it once. There weren't many accounting entries in it. Mostly, it was more like a diary, with a detailed record of the events of daily life. It made me think that it might have been what she turned to for comfort when life was hard.'

Something else that had left a strong impression on Kotoko was the lack of entries for several days following the announcement of the end of the war on 15 August – a telling sign of the turmoil there was at the time.

'The year after the war ended, Shufu no Tomo began a movement called "The League for Continual Use of Kakeibo".'

'Continual use?' Maho laughed.

'Yes. The aim was to gather various statistics through regular keeping of household accounts, even in difficult times. It's thanks to this that a substantial amount of data was collected, of the kind used to calculate Engel's coefficient.'

'I wonder if it became easier to keep a kakeibo when times were better.'

'Not that so much as –' Kotoko turned to look at Maho – 'well, I wonder if it was the act of keeping a kakeibo that made it easier to get through everything somehow.'

'What do you mean?'

'Maybe this is overdramatic, but I think that those housewives who were willing to do their kakeibo during all that turmoil – what I mean is those who were educated and willing enough to do so – became a mainstay of Japan's recovery after the war. Of course there were a number of factors that contributed to recovery. But I do believe that was one.'

'I see what you mean.' Maho smiled at the heatedness with which her grandmother had spoken.

At this point Saho awoke, bringing an end to the conversation. There was no chance for Kotoko to speak about her desire to find work, but it didn't take much to stop her; after all, it was a difficult thing to confess to a grandchild that her pension was insufficient and she was running short of money.

'Come here, pet, come to Granny.' Saho felt warm and heavy in her great-grandmother's arms. For a moment she looked up at Kotoko with clear, sad eyes, then burst into tears. 'Don't cry, Saho, it's Granny.'

Maho tried to take her but Kotoko clung fast to Saho, cradling her. She wished with all her heart that it could always be this easy to take away a child's sorrow and burdens. In that moment, her mind was made up: *I'll try anything*. It was contrary to the counsellor's advice, but life was short and she was only getting older. She did not know how many years she had left to work, and if she could just get started, along the way she might discover the thing that was just right for her.

'Excuse me, is this the number for Kotoko Mikuriya?' said a polite voice when Kotoko answered the phone a few days later. 'Um, it's me, Saito.'

'Sorry, who?'

'Er – sorry, Saito, from the convenience store, in Jujo.'

The store where Kotoko had been interviewed for a job. She did not recognise Saito's voice on the phone.

'I'm sorry to have troubled you the other day,' Kotoko apologised, thinking that this must be why he was calling, since she had been so rude as to waste his time when she was not qualified to work in a convenience store.

'No, no – not at all. I would gladly have hired you if you were in your sixties.'

Kotoko was not amused. Having been rejected by him once already, she did not appreciate having her age brought up again, even if she was an old lady.

'Have you found a job yet?

'No, I haven't.' She told him about going to Hello Work and the counselling session. 'But I've given it a lot of thought and decided I'm willing to try anything. I applied for cleaning services and housekeeping – for what it's worth.' Kotoko laughed self-deprecatingly. 'I don't know if I've got a chance, though.'

'That's good.'

'Why is that good?'

'I'm sorry, I wasn't clear. Actually, the reason I'm calling is to ask your advice.'

'About what?'

'It's about the Minatoya shop, near the south exit of the station.'

Kotoko knew Minatoya, a traditional Japanese confectionery shop that was well known in Jujo, having been in business since after the war. However, it was a long way from the main shopping street and Kotoko did not go there often, but whenever she needed to buy confectionery as a gift, this was where she went.

'Minatoya have finally decided to open a branch in the main street. They've been waiting for the right moment, you see.'

'Are they now. That will be nice. Much more convenient.'

'Apparently they plan to have a *dango* sweet dumpling stall outside the shop front, with a showcase and register inside, and a small area for drinking tea at the rear.'

'Well, that will make it a very nice shop indeed, won't it?'

'They're looking for someone to work at the dumpling stall. Someone steady and old enough, or should I say elderly . . . or perhaps senior citizen – a granny type, in other words.'

'Really,' Kotoko said dryly.

'We were discussing it the other day at the Lions Club. Mr Minato was saying how surprisingly hard it is to find exactly the right kind of old lady. Someone reliable, trim and neat, who would be a good advertisement for Minatoya. When I heard that, I immediately thought of you. Mrs Mikuriya is just the person, I thought.'

'Goodness . . . me? Oh, I'm not—'

'No, you're perfect. You look like a sweet old lady, and you have the ideal background. I already talked to Mr Minato about it, and he was very keen to meet you.'

'But last time – didn't you say I looked young?'

'Oh, but then I was . . .'

Kotoko could almost see Saito scratching his head as he spoke.

'I was, um, on the spot and winging it, and um, might have overdone it a bit. But you will have no problem, because you definitely look sixty-five.'

'You are too honest, you know.'

'Sorry,' Saito said with a laugh. 'But after that interview, you were still on my mind.'

'And why was that?'

'Well, you may be getting on in years, but you had a spark in your eye and seemed very motivated. I was actually thinking of asking you to do the early-morning cleaning shift, but I think you will be more valuable at Minatoya.'

After confirming with Kotoko that it was all right to pass on her contact details, Saito hung up. Kotoko put down the receiver, stunned at how quickly everything had fallen into place. Of course she had not been hired yet, and even if she was, she did not know whether she could do a good job or not. But for the first time in a very long while, she felt needed again. Something she had not felt since her husband had come to buy a handkerchief and ask her to go out with him. The thought moved her to tears.

3

Goal: Save Ten Million Yen!

Maho Ido was entering personal details into her smartphone: name, address, telephone number . . . She'd done it so often that after one tap the rest popped up in autocorrect.

Once she had entered the obligatory information, she answered questions about magazine and web statement preferences. Then she pulled an ATM card from her wallet to refer to while entering the account number for automatic debits. Lastly, she answered questions about her husband's income, current housing status – own home, rental or subsidised housing – loan details if any, deposits and savings. This last section always varied, depending on which credit card company was asking.

Once finished, Maho lightly tapped the button that read *Do you want to proceed with this transaction?* in large letters, and the screen refreshed.

Confirmation will follow by email. If you are not contacted in the next twenty-four hours please call the number below.

Ding! The gentle signal for a new email arriving came almost immediately. Now all she had to do was to send away her 'confirmation of identity' documents.

At this point, Maho let out a sigh. Despite this all being routine for her, she was nervous. The slightest error and she might be too late to receive the benefits, or fail to earn points. She massaged her shoulders and rolled her neck. Between two and three thirty in the afternoon every day, when her three-year-old daughter, Saho, took a nap, was the only time Maho could devote to what she called her 'mini-income'. This was the term popularly used by women's magazines and the like, to describe small amounts of income earned through the internet, piecework or side jobs at home. Magazines and other publications devoted to economising frequently covered the topic since it was something women at home were able to do with relative ease.

Today, Maho calculated, she would earn ¥5,000-worth of points by the end of the month – enough to cover her allowance. However, this month she was also hoping to make a bit extra as next week she would be meeting friends from junior college for lunch at a French restaurant in Omotesando. The meal alone would cost ¥3,800, with drinks and service fee on top of that.

She planned to wear a simple, light-brown, flower-patterned dress that she had bought last autumn for ¥2,000 through a flea-market app. It was several seasons old, but at least the brand was one that all major department stores carried. Taiyo and her parents had complimented her on it and the way it matched the reddish-brown highlights in her hair.

Maho was the only one in her family with natural brown highlights. She'd taken a lot of flak because of it at high school, from teachers who suspected her of dyeing her hair, which was against the rules. But since leaving school it had worked to her advantage, because now she could look reasonably stylish without the cost of going to a beauty salon.

As she hadn't worn the dress in front of her friends yet, Maho had decided that the only thing she needed to buy new were some earrings to go with it. These too she purchased through an app which sold amateur handmade jewellery, and bargained the price down from ¥600 to ¥500. Each earring was a baroque pearl on a gold chain, an imitation of earrings worn by the heroine of a hit TV drama at the end of last year. The real thing would have cost ¥30,000 – way beyond Maho's budget. But they looked adorable on her, swinging from the gold chains to peek through gaps in her hair.

She decided to browse a little longer on Pucci Picci Wallet, her favourite of the websites aimed at housewives looking for side jobs. There were several methods of earning through this site; making online purchases through it, for example, would net her 1% of the cost in points. Responding to questionnaires in exchange for points was, however, probably the most popular method.

Maho's other strategy for earning points was to open bank, brokerage or foreign exchange accounts. Recently she had also been applying for a lot of credit cards, timing her applications to take advantage of campaigns that offered large numbers of points to new users. She almost never used these credit cards. Instead, she kept them all together in one place, then sorted them every six months to close them down and dispose of the cards. She did feel a little bad for the companies who launched these campaigns in order to increase customer numbers, but for her, it was not a bad way to make a bit extra while her daughter was little.

The same was true for the foreign-exchange accounts she opened at the brokerage firms that were springing up like mushrooms nowadays. These places were always touting for customers, and a new account with one could net anything from five thousand to an amazing twenty or thirty thousand points. But there were strict conditions, with the firms requiring anything from ¥100,000 to ¥300,000 to be deposited in the account and then used for trading. On top of which you had to earn the right to receive these points by establishing a performance record, in a process known as 'claiming rights'.

Although Maho had experience of working at a brokerage firm, she knew little about foreign-exchange trading. Some of her colleagues had objected to handling this kind of trade, and one former boss had once even said to her, 'To be honest it's no better than gambling.' Maho therefore conducted such transactions only when she absolutely had to, and would be in a cold sweat every time, as there was always the chance of instantly wiping out several tens of thousands of yen. She created her performance records by plugging in 'sell' and 'buy' at the same time and selling both off immediately. She wrote off the transaction fees, and even if she didn't make a profit, at least she had her performance record.

Credit cards weren't as nerve-racking, but there was a limit to how many times she could apply. Most companies awarded points to new applicants only, and Maho was beginning to run out of cards to apply for.

Trading shares in extremely small amounts and selling off unwanted items on the flea-market app were her other methods of earning money from home while looking after a small child. Maho had an account for share trading with a brokerage firm that did not charge fees on transactions worth less than ¥100,000 per day. She was cautious, watching for the right time to buy relatively stable, well-known brands with shareholder dividends, and sell when they netted a few thousand yen in profit. She would buy around two months before the return date, when she was fairly certain the shares were rising. If they went down before then, she waited until the return date to receive her shareholder dividends. So far, she had not sustained any big losses from this level of activity. Nevertheless, she was careful not to let her money-making activities lean too much towards share trading. Having worked at a brokerage firm, she knew there was no such thing as absolute certainty when it came to shares and investments. Once, she had lost money when a certain company unexpectedly abolished shareholder benefits and their share price plummeted. It would be different if she were single, but since she was using her husband's salary for her transactions, and they had a child to support, plunging their savings into negative figures was something that she absolutely wanted to avoid.

Maho permitted herself an allowance of ¥5,000 per month,

which was enough provided she was able to supplement it with a mini-income ranging from a few thousand to ten thousand yen a month. If she had any money remaining at the end of the month, she put it into savings or aside for emergency use. She wanted to at least earn her own pocket money. It wasn't that she didn't feel entitled to take it from her husband's salary, more that she felt freer to use money however she liked when she had made it for herself, and besides, she liked the challenge of earning it.

Taiyo was a firefighter. He made just over ¥230,000 a month, including overtime. It wasn't a great deal, but at least his job was secure. On the 17th of every month, payday, Maho went to the bank first thing and withdrew ¥45,000 in cash, making sure to change ¥25,000 of this into ¥1,000 bills for food and household expenses. She put this money into the pink wallet which she used for that purpose, and was careful to always keep the housekeeping money separate from money for her personal use.

The pink patent-leather wallet was one she had bought in high school, with money that she had saved and combined with a New Year's money gift from her grandmother. Its edges were slightly worn, but the finish was still shiny. She had yearned for that wallet and been over the moon when, finally, she was able to buy it. That's why she still treasured it today, even though she knew the pink ribbon design was somewhat childish for a woman in her twenties.

Once she arrived home with the cash from the bank, Maho would separate the money for food into five envelopes, each containing four ¥1,000 notes, and keep the remaining ¥5,000 for daily necessities. Each envelope represented one week's worth of food money, and if any remained after the fifth week, she set it aside to buy condiments, or occasionally top up her own allowance.

She allotted Taiyo a monthly allowance of ¥20,000. Until recently it had been ¥10,000, but after he complained – unsurprisingly – she had given him a raise. Every month she handed him his money in an envelope from the bank, on which she wrote 'Thank You', decorated with pictures and stickers by Saho and herself.

A feeling of deep satisfaction would spread through Maho's chest whenever she firmly closed her kakeibo accounting book. On the cover she had written in large letters, *Goal: Save Ten Million Yen!*, an amount she had decided on after reading a women's magazine feature that recommended having this much in savings by the time a first child went to university. It sounded like a good idea to Maho, and was something she could do to feel more secure about the future. Though the idea was borrowed, once written down in her book it became her own. Her inspiration. Achieve this, and all her anxieties about the future would be eased.

They lived on a tight monthly budget, but banking Taiyo's twice-yearly bonus of ¥280,000 enabled her to save ¥1 million per year. There was enough for travel and new electrical equipment as well, and they were not unhappy. But once Saho came along, the only travel they ever did was to a nearby hot spring, and the only big purchase was a crib. Maho strove to save whenever she could and not make any big expenditures.

Whenever she felt discouraged, all she had to do was to look at the cover of her kakeibo to feel reassured.

A peep at the monthly income and expenses for the Ido family would look something like this:

Salary (take-home pay): ¥230,000
Rent: ¥88,000
Food: ¥20,000 (¥4,000 per week x 5 weeks)
Miscellaneous expenses (daily necessities): ¥5,000
Taiyo's allowance: ¥20,000
Smartphone (for two): approx. ¥5,000
Utilities: ¥10,000
Insurance (Taiyo): ¥2,000
Emergencies, leisure, etc.: ¥20,000
Savings: ¥60,000

Rent, utility expenses and the regular monthly saving deposit were all debited automatically. The child allowance from the government went in its entirety into a separate account. There were times when Maho did wish for an extra ¥10,000 or ¥20,000, but for now she was satisfied. Once Saho went to kindergarten, she was thinking of going back to work to pay for kindergarten expenses and so forth.

Maho often made Taiyo's favourite hamburger steak on payday as a way of showing her appreciation for her husband. She made the base by adding a piece of well-drained tofu and canned corn to the ground beef, browned both sides of the hamburger in a frying pan, put cheese on top to melt, then poured boil-in-the-bag hashed-beef stew from the 100-yen shop over as a simmering sauce. The hashed-beef roux became a rich demi-glace sauce that went well with the sweet-corn and cheese.

That evening, her husband, dark from the sun, came home and said cheerfully, 'I'm home,' his voice sounding louder than usual. Maho couldn't help but giggle in the kitchen. Saho also put her hand over her mouth and giggled in imitation of her mother.

'What's this, what are you laughing at?' Taiyo picked up Saho in his arms with a big smile.

'Get changed and wash your hands,' Maho said. 'We're having hamburger steak today.'

'*To-chan*, today hamburg.'

Maho had taught Saho to call her *Mama*, the English loan word for Mum that was most commonly used amongst her generation, but for some reason Taiyo preferred To-chan, the old-fashioned Japanese word for Daddy. Apparently, it had always been his dream to be called this. Since he himself called his own parents Mama and Papa, Maho suspected his preference for To-chan might be an affectation, somewhat like giving a pet dog a pretentious Japanese name such as Wasabi or Azuki. Maho picked up Saho in her arms and jiggled her playfully. 'Why don't the two of you have a shower now?' she called to her husband, who was heading for the washroom in high spirits.

Taiyo made a non-committal sound in reply. He was a happy man.

*

'Wow!' When Koharu showed her engagement ring, Maho and her friends oohed and aahed loudly.

They were at a backstreet French restaurant in upmarket Omotesando on Saturday, celebrating Koharu's engagement with champagne – or sparkling water for Maho – and the ¥3,800 lunch course.

Koharu's ring sparkled beneath the restaurant chandelier. It was a Tiffany creation, consisting of a large heart-shaped diamond surrounded by smaller diamonds.

'These are one- and two-carat diamonds,' Koharu said, sounding as if she could barely suppress her awe. The diamond ring looked as if it might fall off her slender finger.

'Oh, would it be too crass to ask how much it cost then?' said Nami, with a smile. Nami was usually the bluntest and most talkative of the four, but to her old friends' eyes, the smile was a little wry.

'Of course you can ask,' said Koharu, smiling even wider in response. But she didn't answer the question. She looked like a celebrity, hedging questions at a public appearance to announce an engagement.

'Did Kotaro buy that for you?' Ikuno asked tentatively. Ikuno worked in the accounting department of a small food company in Tokyo. She had always had good grades, but was quiet and not much given to showing her emotions. Currently, she was also studying to be a licensed tax accountant.

'Yeah.' Koharu inclined her slender neck, as if uncertain. 'Well, I'm not sure. I didn't ask. But I suspect his parents might've helped.'

As far as the others were aware, Koharu's fiancé was an

ordinary salaried worker. When Koharu had first told them about meeting Kotaro at a matchmaking party after she entered the workforce, her friends had been far more interested in such details as his height, weight, looks and employer. The fact that his parents ran a large construction company in an out-of-the-way place in rural Chiba Prefecture was a nugget of information they had not paid much attention to at the time, and it had certainly never occurred to them that it would make this kind of difference once the pair became engaged.

In addition to the ring, Koharu's in-laws-to-be had apparently also purchased an off-the-plan condominium for the couple in a soon-to-be-built tower at Toyosu in central Tokyo. 'But they're only paying for the flat itself,' Koharu told them. 'We have to pay the monthly maintenance fee and reserve fund contributions, which will be quite a burden.'

Even so, that'd be less than my monthly rent, and *she gets to live in a luxury condo with more than a hundred square metres in a prime location in Toyosu,* thought Maho.

'Oh, I know the condo tower you mean. Is that one where a place goes for two hundred million by any chance?' Nami had no compunction about asking. She worked for a real-estate company and was familiar with property prices.

In junior college Koharu had been tall and slender, with a nice figure, but not what you'd call outstanding in looks. Her appearance changed dramatically, however, when she started working for a department store and was assigned to the out-of-store sales department. She began to wear good suits that accentuated her height and make-up that brought out her features, making her look like an exotic Asian model from abroad. Her long hair upped her feminine charm factor even more. When she met her fiancé at a matchmaking party, he had aggressively pursued her. Their wedding was to be held at an ultra-luxurious hotel in the trendy Ebisu district of Tokyo, to be followed by a ten-day honeymoon in Italy. *No doubt that would also be an extravaganza, travelling business class and staying in super-luxurious hotels,* thought Maho. She gave a series of small sighs – discreetly – so that no one would notice.

'Hey, how's Saho? She must be getting big,' Nami asked Maho as they were finishing the main course of chicken confit. After hearing about Koharu's engagement all through appetiser, salad, soup and main course, the question might have been aimed more to shift the topic from Koharu's glamorous wedding than from an actual desire to hear about Saho's progress.

'Getting bigger. She's already three.' Maho dug out the best of recent photos of Saho on her smartphone for everyone to see. It had been taken the previous Sunday, and showed Taiyo pushing Saho on the swing at the park.

'Aww, look at her.'

'She's so . . .'

Nami and Ikuno exclaimed loudly, but Koharu merely looked at it with an aloof smile. This was the only expression Maho had seen on Koharu's face ever since she became engaged, and Maho could never tell what she really thought.

'So . . . what?' Maho asked with a smile.

Nami sighed heavily. 'I remember her hands were like tiny maple leaves when she was born. It makes me emotional to see her big enough to ride on a swing by herself now. What have I been doing all that time?'

Maho recalled the three of them visiting a few days after she had given birth. Her friends had taken turns to hold Saho, and touch and stroke her cheeks.

'You've built up a career, haven't you, Nami?'

This year Nami had qualified as a registered real estate broker, and was also working hard to become a certified interior designer. Nami's dream was to build a condominium designed entirely by herself.

'Taiyo's still a clean-cut, good-looking guy,' Ikuno said, her eyes on the photo. Maho tittered coyly. She was secretly proud of her firefighter husband, who worked out every day, and still had a strong, powerful physique. They had been high-school sweethearts, both marrying their first love.

Saho's nose took after her father's, and together the pair looked handsome enough to be in a commercial for dish-washing detergent.

'When I first heard that you planned to get married at twenty-three to a man the same age, I honestly wondered why you would choose to do that. But seeing this photo now of your adorable daughter, I can understand.'

Nami and Ikuno looked at each other and nodded in agreement. Maho was stunned. It took a moment for it to sink in what she had just heard. She froze.

'Yes. I was so impressed at you being able to make that kind of decision at the time. Seeing Saho now, it wasn't such a bad one, I think.'

The two looked genuinely impressed.

'I mean you gave up your job and all, to gamble everything on that husband. That was amazing.'

Is that what they'd thought? Maho could no longer taste the apple and apricot crème chiboust in her mouth.

The only diamond Maho possessed was a very small necklace. Taiyo had given it to her when she was a student, with money he saved from his part-time job. The design was very sweet – three small diamonds strung together like a shooting star – and Maho had been thrilled to receive it: Taiyo didn't have much money, and yet he had given her an expensive gift. They didn't buy an engagement ring. She knew that Taiyo didn't have the money for that, and she was satisfied with the diamond necklace. Besides, one of the older women at work had told her that 'you only wear an engagement ring for a short time, and never wear it once you have a child', which sounded sensible enough advice to Maho.

Instead, they bought two simple Cartier wedding rings to give each other. Though Maho liked this ring a great deal, her heart nevertheless thudded when she was presented with the sight of Koharu's large heart-shaped diamond. *I want that*, she thought. She wanted to try it on and stare at its sparkles. To wear it somewhere and be told, 'Oh, how lovely.' To put it in her jewellery box and gaze at it sometimes. She'd never had such a thought before now. Generally, she wasn't that interested in jewellery, and was usually too busy to even look at it in department stores.

But the sight of this diamond made Maho realise that until

you actually see something up close, you never really know what you feel about it.

Seeing Koharu's large diamond made her own necklace seem like a collection of scrap by comparison. The diamonds in her necklace were probably even smaller than the ones surrounding the large heart-shaped diamond in Koharu's ring. Until today it had been her most prized piece of jewellery, which she only wore on special occasions, but it would have paled in the presence of Koharu's ring, and Maho was heartily glad that she hadn't worn it to the French restaurant. Buying diamond jewellery was not a realistic proposition for her, and Maho knew that in time she would get over her envy. However, Nami and Ikuno's words continued to sting. Oblivious, they continued innocently:

'I was surprised that you got married so soon after you started work, too, and then quit so readily.'

'I couldn't do that.'

'Me neither. I still have things I want to do, workwise and relationship-wise.'

'I knew Maho was amazing.'

'If it were me, I'd probably wonder if there wasn't somebody better out there.'

While they did sound genuinely impressed on the one hand, after Koharu's story it sounded to Maho as if they were also saying: *How could you quit your job for a husband with such a low monthly salary?*

She should have come back straight away, and said something like, 'Hey, what do you mean!' Then she could have figured out what they really meant, and not been left brooding. But she didn't, and now that she knew what her friends had really thought about her marriage, she was left feeling uncomfortable.

Hearing Koharu's story jogged Maho's memory of her own lead-up to marriage, and the dreams she had had back then. Maho and Taiyo did not have an overseas honeymoon. Instead, they bought budget air tickets to Okinawa and simply drove around the main island by car. Of course they did eat a lot of cheap but delicious food, and had one romantic night in a cottage at a seaside hotel, but Maho's dream had been to go to Hawaii. Taiyo had just started working at the time, however, and could not take much time off, but it was the cost more than anything and thoughts of what they would need for their new life ahead, which made them reluctant to spend a large sum on their honeymoon.

Ever since, Maho had dreamed vaguely of going to Hawaii one day. A dream she was constantly reminded of because it was featured so often in housewives' magazines. Careful examination of these magazines also led Maho to the conclusion that, as a holiday destination, Hawaii was very cost-effective. For one thing, you could take beautiful photos that showed to advantage on Twitter and Instagram; secondly, you could buy famous souvenirs that would please everybody, and thirdly – and in a sense perhaps the biggest reason of all – it was somewhere that would provoke moderate envy. But not special enough to cause too much ill will or jealousy.

Of course it cost money, but Maho honestly believed that just one holiday in Hawaii would be far more satisfying, to her and her friends, than any number of trips to hot springs deep in the mountains, or minor Asian resorts.

She could picture herself: young mother in a long sundress with small child, playing in the waves on a white sandy beach . . . What a great photo that would make. Simply thinking of it sent her into a daydream. She also wanted to eat breakfast in a restaurant beside the sea, and buy cute, inexpensive children's clothes. Apparently in Hawaii you could buy lots of reasonably priced designer-brand clothes that weren't available in Japan. Then there was all the food to be had from the food vans that everyone talked about: she wanted to try garlic shrimp, and Malassada, the deep-fried doughnuts you could buy in Hawaii. She also wanted a Louis Vuitton purse from the duty-free store. Louis Vuitton was often featured in housewives' magazines; a luxury brand that was casual and timeless – she could use it for ever regardless of trends. Maho used her wallets for ten years, so it wouldn't be expensive in the long run. There was also the option, though it was not something she voiced out loud, of pawning or selling it on a flea-market site if she ever tired of it or ran out of money. The Vuitton brand had a high conversion rate.

Maho had long stopped dwelling on this dream. Daily life was far too busy. But still something weighed on her that she couldn't exactly pin down. Was her vague idea to save ¥10 million for Saho really the right course of action? There had to be other ways of living, to use money as a means to enjoy her life now.

Twice a week she went to the supermarket, as she had decided, but while there, was always mentally calculating the total cost of everything in the basket. For several years now she had not been able to go shopping and buy things without looking at the price first, or without a plan. Almost from the start, she had given up on spending large sums of money.

Saho no longer pleaded for candy or toys at the supermarket like other children. She knew there was no chance that Maho would buy them for her. Was that the kind of life she really wanted?

'What? Are you having regrets about getting married?' Miho asked straight out the following Saturday when she was over visiting.

'I didn't say that. It's just . . .'

'To tell the truth I was surprised you quit your job when you got married.'

'Huh?'

'Women don't do that any more. Or at least they stay until they have a baby.'

'Well, Taiyo did night shifts, so it was hard to keep the same hours,' Maho mumbled, repeating what she had told everyone when she first married.

Actually, there was another reason, which her sister and family didn't know about. The truth was that she hated her job at the securities firm, with its strict quotas and constant pressure to sell and solicit new customers. At the end of each month she would have to call one of her few customers and say, 'Mr Sato, you have 1.2 million in MMFs. How about converting it into Australian dollars? There's a fund that uses bonds issued by a Japanese automobile company, which has an interest rate as high as 5.5 per cent. Now is also a good time to buy Australian dollars.' Et cetera. Maho really struggled to bring herself to say this kind of thing. It might have been easier if the fund really was profitable, but at the time the yen was extremely strong, stock prices were low, and it was definitely not a good time to buy either Australian or American dollars. Nevertheless, she was still required to pressure her clients, even when they were also aware of the state of things. She had to achieve her quota. When bankers recommended funds with poor terms to her grandmother, Maho could not blame them, because it was what she used to do. She had quickly realised after joining the company that she was not cut out to work in sales. Only Taiyo knew how she felt about her job. She had been crying over it one night on a date, when he said, 'You could marry me and quit your job.' Overjoyed, she had said yes, but it was not very exciting or romantic to tell people that 'I was complaining about my quotas so he asked me to marry him and so she had never told anyone.

'In that case it's not a problem, is it? If that's what Taiyo's job is like,' Miho responded coolly.

'I guess so. Still . . .' Maho said.

'It's nothing to care about.'

But it wasn't the only reason Maho had married, so she did care.

'Anyway, I'm thinking about moving,' Miho changed the subject.

'You're kidding.' Maho looked at Miho, who blushed and smiled self-consciously. 'Really?'

'Yes, really.'

'Where?'

'Around here . . . Jujo, I mean'

'For real? But – why?'

Miho's gaze shifted to Saho as she spoke. 'After what you said, I did a lot of thinking and study, too. I went to seminars on economising and investing – stuff like that – and study group breakfast meetings.'

'That's great.'

'Yeah. And what I discovered was, everywhere I went, they said much the same thing as you. Review fixed costs, save small amounts, that kind of thing.'

'What? For real?'

'Yeah, it's true. This is kind of hard to say, but I have to admit you're pretty amazing, Sis. What you taught me is actually really useful.'

'Hey, what's up with you? You're being very nice today,' Maho teased, but deep down she was happy. Happy that her little sister, from whom she'd felt distant ever since Miho entered the workforce, would praise her this way.

'So anyway, I'm thinking to look for somewhere else to live.'

'Oh wow, I'm so glad. I'll be able to see more of you, and you can take care of Saho for me.'

'Hey, don't get too excited.' Miho frowned, then quickly smiled again and laughed.

Grandma. Maho was rooted to the spot. She still became teary at the sight of her grandmother seated outside the traditional

Japanese confectionery *wagashi* shop, midway down the shopping mall.

'Gran-gran, dah!' Saho called loudly, unaware of her mother's feelings. She stretched out her tiny fingers to point, 'Dah, Grandma!' and turned to look proudly at Maho. Maho wondered if Saho was proud of being the first to spot her great-grandmother, or proud of her working here.

When Kotoko, Maho's grandmother, announced that she had a job selling sweet dumplings at a wagashi shop in the shopping mall, serving not behind the counter inside but at a stall out front, her family and relatives had all been in a state of shock, Maho's parents most of all. Her father was so stunned by the news he could not speak for some time.

Miho, however, took it matter-of-factly, and went to her grandmother's house one evening to talk with her at length. 'It's all right,' she reported back to the family over LINE and email. 'Grandma used to work on the sales floor in a Ginza department store before she married.'

Maho hadn't known that her grandmother had had such a glamorous job when she was young. Learning about it made her slightly more comfortable with the idea of her working now. She knew her grandmother as a good cook and a reliable presence in her life, but Maho had never pictured her grandmother's life, much less before her marriage. Grandma had once been in her twenties, too, so there was nothing odd about her having been an attractive sales girl. She wanted to think of this new job as an opportunity to learn more about her grandmother. But upon actually seeing her at the shop with a scarf covering her hair, Maho was lost for words. Tears rose in her eyes.

'Mummy cry? What's wrong, Mummy?'

Maho quickly wiped her tears, but to her chagrin they continued to flow.

Kotoko wore a uniform-like navy-blue smock. Maho could accept herself or Miho wearing such a uniform, but the sight of her grandmother in one was confronting. It was shocking to see her usually stylish Grandma – always so dignified and refined, but with an innocence as well – looking so small and frail in cheap work clothes.

'What's the matter, Maho? Don't forget there are customers,' Kotoko had chided Maho gently but firmly the first time. To Maho, she looked distressingly like a small child doing its first grown-up errand. Maho and Saho went to visit her sometimes now when she was working on the weekends or Wednesdays, and although she was getting used to seeing her grandmother at the shop, the sight of her from afar never failed to catch at Maho's heart.

'Hello, Maho and Saho,' Kotoko greeted them with a big smile.

'Grandma, do you have time for a tea break?'

'I do at two o'clock.'

'Would you like to meet us? We can do some shopping until then.'

'That'd be nice. I'll see you at that coffee shop.'

When Maho and Saho had finished their errands, they went to the coffee shop to find Kotoko already waiting, minus the uniform and scarf.

Her eyes were shining and her cheeks had a glow in them. She was, to put it mildly, looking in rude good health.

'How are you, Grandma? You're not tired? Are you okay?' Maho couldn't help asking. She still worried.

'Not in the least. I don't have to be on my feet all the time, you know. I can sit down and serve the customers, so it's very easy. All I do is sit, smile and talk to customers. At the end of the day, I go home without any of the tedious work like closing the cash register or daily reports to do. It's so easy I almost feel guilty being paid. *And* I can take home leftover sweets and *inari* sushi as well.'

Maho had heard that in addition to Grandma, two other elderly ladies were working at the shop, and they all took different shifts. Apparently, Grandma was currently receiving a trainee's pay of ¥900 per hour, which would go up to ¥1,000 an hour next month.

'Come and see me at home soon. I've got lots of okaki rice crackers from the shop past their use-by date.'

'I'm glad it all seems to be going well.' Maho was relieved. Remembering the fuss that Grandma's new job had caused in the Mikuriya household, she couldn't help adding, 'Dad still can't accept it.'

Her father had been angry about his mother finding a job without telling him, and apparently even told Maho's mother that it was an embarrassment for him to have an aged parent standing outside a shop in the mall.

'How can he? If I hadn't worked at the department store, I would never have met his father, and he wouldn't have been born. Why's he so upset now?'

'Well, I guess he just doesn't like the idea,' Maho said, 'from his perspective, I mean.'

Until her grandmother started working, Maho had known nothing about her grandparents' relationship. Now she knew that they had been a love match, which was rare in those days. To her father, however, that and this were two different things.

'You quit your job when you married, didn't you, Grandma?' she asked abruptly.

'Of course.'

'Didn't you regret it?'

'That's how it was in those days. We didn't even think about working after marriage. If you told your boss you were getting married, it was the same as saying that you were going to quit.'

'I guess so,' said Maho nodding as she sipped her iced coffee. She looked down.

'What is it? Did something happen?'

'To tell the truth ...' Maho told her grandmother about Koharu's engagement and the series of conversations with her friends. 'I don't know ... It just made me think, I suppose.'

'About your own employment situation? Or Koharu's engagement?'

'Both, I think. I was surprised that getting married could be like that, I suppose – everything falling onto her plate – and then it was a shock to find out what my friends really thought about my marriage.' Maho continued in a low voice, muttering the thing she did not want to admit even to herself. 'I just know they were comparing me to Koharu, and thinking how the choice of a husband can really change who a woman is. On the one hand, there's Koharu with a tower condominium in Toyosu, and on the other, me in a flat in Jujo.'

'You shouldn't talk like that. Taiyo is a good man, and you're doing a fine job bringing up Saho. I think you're happy.'

'Of course, I know that. I know it, but I still feel sad, somehow.'

'Remember I mentioned Motoko Hani and kakeibo the other day?'

'Oh, the woman your grandmother said was strict?'

'Yes. But she said many wise things, one of which was her recommendation to use the kakeibo for planning and scheduling.'

'To make plans in the family budget book?'

'Yes. She always maintained that a kakeibo was not just to record spending; scheduling is also important. How much money do you have coming in this month, how much going out? How much of that can I use for myself? She said it was necessary to have a grasp of these things.'

'Amazing.'

'Unlike me, you have more leeway to make plans, Maho. At least, you have a definite plan for up until Saho starts work, don't you? I think it would be a good idea to draw up a plan of when, where, and how much money you will spend in the next twenty years or so. Then have another careful think about how much you need. Once you've done that, maybe you can spare yourself any useless anxiety, and stop comparing yourself to others.'

'Yes, Grandma.'

It was such sound, reassuring advice. However, Maho couldn't help picking up on a minor phrase. 'What do mean "unlike me"? Are you saying you can't predict your future?'

'Well, of course not. I could keel over tomorrow.'

In spite of her grandmother's mischievous smile, something didn't add up for Maho. 'But if you went tomorrow, you wouldn't need money, would you?'

Kotoko gave a small sigh. 'Well, to be honest, I'm a bit worried about the future.'

'Why? What do you mean?'

Her grandmother had always been a picture of calm and serenity to Maho. She lived in a nice house, had good furniture and crockery, did her budgeting in her kakeibo and led a good life. She was always there, a constant and close presence for Maho and the Mikuriya household – the ideal grandmother. Maho was proud of her.

'I don't know how much I'll need in future. My pension was reduced after your grandfather died, and it's not that I don't have any savings, but if I break into them now and then need nursing care later on, I'll be in trouble.'

'So that's why you wanted to work again!'

'Of course I did want to go back to work, but it is true that I am also a little short of money.'

Maho did not know what to say.

'Nobody in the family knows about this, but I'm glad I could tell you, Maho. I may need help one day, but until then I want to get by on my own as much as possible. Please don't tell your mother or father.'

'I won't. But I do think you should tell them yourself soon.'

'Don't worry, I'll tell them. Besides, it's not as if I've run out of money. I'm still okay.'

It was true, Maho knew. When they had talked about

savings interest rates earlier, Grandma had said she had ¥10 million in savings.

'I understand. Let me know if there's anything I can do to help. I'll do whatever I can.'

'I enjoy working and feel happy every day – that's the truth,' Grandma said, with a smile that looked genuine to Maho.

The call came late at night. Maho and her family were asleep, being early risers and usually in bed by ten. Taiyo jumped up to answer first, waking up Maho as he did.

'Not mine,' he mumbled sleepily, looking at his smartphone.

'What?' Maho reacted as a vibrating sound replaced the ring. Taiyo was always the one to receive calls in the middle of the night. Startled, Maho scrabbled for her phone near her pillow. The caller ID on the screen read *Koharu*.

'Maho?'

Maho was even more astonished to hear Koharu sobbing on the other end of the line. 'Koharu?'

'I'm so sorry, I'm so sorry.'

'What is it? What's wrong?'

'Can I come and see you now?' Koharu asked through her tears.

'Sure . . . are you alone? Where are you?'

'In Ginza . . . I'll get a taxi. I'm so sorry.'

'Everything okay?' Taiyo had got up and put a cardigan over his pyjamas.

'Something's happened to Koharu. She's on her way here now. I'll close the door, so don't worry, just go back to sleep.'

Taiyo told her to wake him if necessary and went back to

burrow under the duvet. Fortunately, Saho was still asleep on her futon between Maho and Taiyo.

The front door of Maho's apartment gave immediately onto the kitchen and dining table – the only place they could sit and talk. Maho was embarrassed at the thought of how it must compare to Koharu's apartment in the condominium tower, but that couldn't be helped. It was still cold, despite the arrival of spring. Maho turned on the kerosene heater, made hot tea and waited. Eventually there came a discreet knock at the door. She opened it and Koharu stood there with red eyes.

'What's up? Are you okay?'

'Yes.' Koharu gave an embarrassed smile.

Perhaps she calmed down in the taxi, thought Maho. 'What happened?'

Koharu sighed loudly once she'd sat down at the table. 'I, um ... I'm thinking of breaking my engagement,' she said, taking a sip of the tea Maho had poured.

'What? I knew it had to be something major,' Maho said, with a quiver of anticipation as to what that could possibly be.

'They were about to insure me for a huge sum of money, without my knowledge.'

'What? What do you mean?'

According to Koharu, as soon as she'd become engaged, she had been asked to hand over her personal name seal and identity Individual Number Card. Then tonight, at a dinner with her fiancé and his parents at a high-class restaurant in Ginza, they had tried to force her to sign insurance papers naming her fiancé and parents-in-law as beneficiaries of an expensive life insurance policy.

'For how much?' asked Maho.

'A hundred million.'

The diamond on the ring finger of Koharu's left hand sparkled ominously.

'What! They might be doing it for your benefit though. I know a large life insurance policy sounds like something out of a murder mystery, but ultimately it's a future guarantee.'

'That's what they said, too. Look – we bought you an apartment in the tower condominium. We do all kinds of business, and it's perfectly normal to have insurance in case something happens.'

'Yes, that's right.'

'But I don't know. I asked if Kotaro had insurance too, and he said, of course, but he told me I'm not the beneficiary. So then I asked, very casually, if I would be made the beneficiary when we married, and he got angry. He said that was a terrible thing to say. Don't you think that's strange?'

'I see what you mean,' said Maho. She didn't feel she could pass judgement on the parents too much. But she did understand why Koharu felt the way she did.

'I thought his mother was so elegant, then all of a sudden it was like she became a different person. She wouldn't forgive me when I apologised, while Kotaro pretended not to see and didn't take my side at all. In the end I just walked out of the restaurant.'

'Aha, so that's what happened.'

'Is it normal for parents-in-law to behave like that? I thought you could tell me since you're married, and know a lot about insurance.'

'Hmm, it's hard to say – every family is different.'

'What do you think, Maho? Do you think I'll be okay if I marry him?'

Maho didn't know how to answer. If she were honest, she did not think that this was something to break off an engagement over. She didn't know why Koharu's fiancé's parents would take out an expensive life insurance policy on her, but maybe that's what some families did. Surely they weren't planning to murder their daughter-in-law for the insurance payout? What she was concerned about, was their treating Koharu as if she were a piece of property, and the fact that Kotaro did not defend her to his parents. But there wasn't enough conclusive proof to answer Koharu's question definitively.

'How about discussing it with Kotaro,' was the best Maho could come up with. A standard answer to be sure, but she did believe that nothing was more important. 'Tell him everything, Koharu. How surprised you were when his parents said that, ask what their intentions are, and let him know you wish he'd taken your side. If he doesn't understand your feelings once you've told him everything then you should reconsider.'

Maho didn't know what Kotaro thought or felt. Maybe he simply didn't realise that Koharu wanted him to take her side.

'How was it when you married, Maho? Did you have any fights, or second thoughts?'

'We were going out for a long time, and I'd known his parents since high school.'

'Oh, yeah, that's right. I'm envious.'

This was a surprise to Maho. How could Koharu, with her mini-celebrity engagement, be jealous of her?

'But it's not as though I didn't feel unsure about marrying.'

'Really! But I thought you were always deeply in love.'

'I had a lot of other stuff going on, too. Like, I said yes to the marriage because I wanted to quit my job. I never told anyone this, but I wasn't very good at it. I couldn't achieve my quotas at the securities firm, and when I complained about it, Taiyo said, "Let's get married." Your story is more romantic than mine.'

'No way.'

They looked at each other and laughed.

'I always thought you were such a rock, Maho, so solid and happy, and you thought my engagement was a joke because it was just play, and not real at all.'

'No, I didn't. I was jealous of you.' Maho suddenly remembered her grandmother's smile.

'There's no such thing as rock solid, in any kind of life.'

'I guess so.'

They talked for a while longer, then Koharu left. Taiyo came out to the kitchen while Maho was cleaning up.

'Sorry, did I wake you?'

'No.'

'Did you hear?'

'Yes. Just a bit.' Taiyo gave Maho a bear hug from behind as she washed the cups. His chin nestled against her cheek. 'It wasn't because of your complaining.'

'What?'

'The reason I proposed. It wasn't because you complained.'

'But – at the time.'

'I'd been wanting to propose for ages, so when you said that, I went with the flow.'

'Seriously?'

'Yep,' he said, bashfully then quickly made for bed. 'Good night!'

Maho stood there laughing to herself. Taiyo was so sweet ... She wished there were someone she could brag about this to.

4

Cost-Effectiveness

Yasuo Komori was having a quiet cigarette on the docks of the small fishing port where he was staying. He blew a puff of smoke out to sea.

'Aren't you partying any more?' a young woman's voice came from behind.

Before he could decide whether or not to respond, Yasuo felt a warm body bump up against his back. It was quite arousing to be hugged from behind by a soft, nice-smelling woman, he noted.

A few days earlier, Yasuo had started working at a seafood factory, in a casual live-in job packing the daily catch of saury into cardboard boxes for shipping. It was still early in the season and today's catch had been small, so the working day had finished by 3 p.m. The seasonal workers, who were accommodated in a dormitory by the sea, immediately began drinking.

'Oy, oy, Rena – have you had too much?'

'Yeeesh, I have.'

Rena was an alluring, long-limbed university student with soft brown-tinted hair. Yasuo guessed her to be around twenty. He didn't know enough about her to even know what the characters were in her name. She was gorgeous-looking and he could tell from her clothes and manner of speaking that she came from a wealthy background. There must have been something lacking or unsatisfactory in her life, however, for her to choose to do hard, back-breaking labour that left you stinking of fish at the end of the day. Yasuo was familiar with the type, though.

Deftly untangling her hands, he – not unkindly – pulled away, remembering to give a hollow laugh at the same time.

'Aren't you going to join in, Komori-san?'

'This old man has had enough.'

'You're not old. Youth is not a time of life, it is a state of mind.'

'Hahahaha.' Yasuo knew that she was quoting the poem *Youth* by Samuel Ullman, but it left him cold. She was probably just parroting some elderly professor from uni. Yasuo wanted to tell such people to decline their pension if they wanted to pretend to be young. But he laughed, feigning ignorance, because he did not want to be drawn in further. 'I'm an old man in mind, too,' he muttered to himself, 'who's nearly forty.'

Rena gently pulled the cigarette from Yasuo's lips and put it in her own. 'Nice,' she said, narrowing her eyes at him.

Spare me, please, he thought. But remembering that there

was a time when he wouldn't have hesitated to go straight to bed with her, he couldn't be too harsh.

'Komori-san, you're different to everyone else.'

'Different – how?'

'The way you think? You have an air about you – I don't know, kinda relaxed?'

'I'm an old man, you know.'

It hadn't been so long ago – two or three years, perhaps – that Yasuo used to pair off with an agreeable girl at every place he worked in his various seasonal jobs. He'd lived like that for nearly ten years, even with a steady girlfriend, until he started going out seriously with Kinari Motoki.

'Do you have a girlfriend?' Rena asked.

Yes, it would be easy to answer, but there was a part of him that wanted to leave her out of this. *It's not that,* he wanted to say. *It's not because I have a girlfriend that I don't want to be with you, I just don't want to do this kind of thing any more.* But he couldn't find the right words.

'Yes, but . . .'

There was no but. He had a girlfriend. Things had got a little weird with Kinari just before this latest job, but Yasuo thought it likely they were still together. *'I want to marry you, Yasuo, or rather, I want a child. Worst-case scenario, just the child is okay. You went to a fairly good university, you're smart, kind, and I like your looks. It's not a bad gene pool.'*

My genes, huh? Typical Kinari to be so straightforward.

He understood that it was natural for a woman in her thirties to want a child, but had never anticipated his relationship with Kinari developing to the point where she wanted his genes. She had been around the same age as Rena when they first met, and they had been together on and off for almost ten years now. Initially, he had her pegged as a young uni student with whom he could have a relationship that would not sour later on. Yasuo was already in his late twenties by then, and finding women his own age to be a bit too full on for him.

They had met in India, at an inn near the Ganges in Varanasi. Yasuo and the other travellers all followed the same daily routine. After being awoken by the sound of bells and prayers, they would head down the still-dark alleys to the river and watch the sun rise over a cup of chai. Then, after contemplating the river for a while, Yasuo would go back to the inn to eat breakfast, chat with other travellers and play cards until around noon. In the evenings he went back to the river to drink chai before returning to the inn for dinner and more chat. He had been passing the days in this fashion for several months when Kinari arrived on the scene.

'How can you lead such an unproductive life!' she always berated Yasuo and the others. Although said with a smile and without rancour, her voice was so loud that it sounded like she was yelling at them. Kinari herself had upon arrival immediately begun touring the ancient sites. Yasuo assumed that once she was done, she would leave, or chill out and join the group of chatterers, like everyone else who came here. But she did neither, and after completing one round of the sights, began going around again. Almost nobody did that.

Essentially it boiled down to the fact that Kinari liked India, but wasn't interested in sitting around idly. She was a strange one, Yasuo had thought. One day, on a whim, he asked her if she wanted to accompany him to Kathmandu, and she accepted without demur. It turned out that it was not India or Varanasi that Kinari was taken with so much as Yasuo himself. After that they continued to meet sporadically, until reaching a new level of intimacy a few years ago, so that now they celebrated each other's birthdays and went back and forth between each other's homes.

This was the woman who was asking for his genes. *It's all Kotoko Mikuriya and her grandchild's fault,* thought Yasuo. *What would that refined old lady have to say if I said to her, Kotoko, lately I don't feel like having sex with young women any more, even when they throw themselves at me. What's wrong with me?* Yasuo snorted with laughter at the thought.

'Komori-san, what are you laughing at? Did I shay something funny?' Rena slurred.

No, but if you'd been thinking, you might have asked, Oh, are you thinking of your girlfriend now? Yasuo wanted to tell her. *You're so confident of your youth and good looks, you can only think of yourself.* Her presence annoyed him even more.

He pictured Kotoko answering his question without so much as turning a hair. *Oh, that's just an age thing, you should see a doctor,* which cracked him up even more.

'What's so funny?' Rena pouted.

'Nothing.' It was too much bother explaining the joke to a girl who was pretending to be drunker than she actually was, and against his better judgement, Yasuo reached for her slender wrist.

*

Just before this latest stint at the seafood factory, Yasuo and Kinari had paid a visit to the apartment of Maho Ido, Kotoko's granddaughter. Yasuo had begun asking Kotoko to water his garden and air the house whenever he was away for work or travel, preferring not to bother Kinari with it as she was also often absent from home for work.

His friendship with Kotoko had continued in this neighbourly vein for a while until recently, when she invited him to visit at her granddaughter's house. 'Maho wants to meet you, too,' she had told him.

Yasuo would have been thrilled if she were single, but Maho had a husband and child to boot. The husband, moreover, was a brawny, tanned and hard-working 29-year-old firefighter. In other words, that pillar of respectability, the public servant. The couple also had a 3-year-old daughter, who Yasuo could tell from photographs would be quite a looker in fifteen years or so. How could he show his face in the home of such a perfect family as that?

And so, on the spur of the moment, he had invited Kinari to go too, since she happened to be with him when he received the invitation from Kotoko by LINE message. 'Take me, too,' she said when he showed it to her, 'I want to meet Kotoko.'

Kinari had followed a more regular career track than Yasuo. She had joined a big travel agency after graduating from university, but left after five years to become a writer, concentrating mainly on travel articles. She hadn't sold a lot, but had written a book entitled *Solo Women Living in Resorts*. Yasuo reasoned that someone in Kinari's line of work was socially adept enough to negotiate any awkwardness in his visit to the Idos', but things turned out better than he could have hoped. Kinari and Maho Ido took to each other immediately, talking easily like old friends about work, travel, even pay cheques and financial planning for old age.

'You want to go to Hawaii? I know a holiday rental house that's great for a family. It's a little far from Waikiki, but that makes it cheaper, and it's still close to the shopping centre.'

'Really? That'd be brilliant. But we probably couldn't stay more than three nights. Is that okay?'

'Strictly speaking, the minimum rental is a week, but I know the owner so I could put in a word.'

'We can't speak English, either.'

'No problem. The owner's wife is third-generation Japanese-American, and speaks a bit of Japanese. I could do the reservation for you.'

'Wow, thank you.'

It was apparent that each immediately recognised the other as someone they could talk to.

'How do people in your employment situation manage with social welfare benefits, Kinari?' Maho asked, after Kinari had first asked about the life of government employees.

'Well, since I'm freelance, I don't get a retirement benefit, and my only pension is from the National Pension Plan, which isn't a lot, so it is a bit of a worry.'

'Yeah, I can imagine.'

'That's why I also have a private defined contribution pension plan – iDeCo it's called.'

'Oh, I've heard of iDeCo. It opened up to public servants as well, recently. I was wondering what it's like.'

'It's tax-deductible so I can totally recommend it.'

'It is?'

'I'm creating my own retirement payout by putting money into the Small Business Mutual Aid Association (SMBA). Those contributions are also tax-deductible and the interest rate is slightly better than at some places.'

'Oh, I didn't know that.'

'At the moment I pay in the maximum possible contributions to both. Being freelance is fraught with uncertainty, and I don't know how long I can keep doing this, so I contribute as much as I can while I'm able. I'm even looking forward a bit to old age.'

'That's nice to hear,' Kotoko interjected. She had been listening to the young people's conversation with a happy smile. 'Being prepared for old age is a good thing – you can't do too much.'

Really? You won't regret later not spending your money now? How can you be sure there'll be no deathbed regrets, wishing you'd spent it after all? Yasuo kept these thoughts to himself, and continued to listen with a smile. He himself did not pay into any kind of defined contribution pension plan, or contribute to a mutual aid fund, he did not even pay into his national pension. Not to mention that his national health insurance had expired.

'I'm so glad that Yasuo is with someone as sensible as you,' Kotoko said, narrowing her eyes meaningfully.

Yasuo, meanwhile, was hearing about Kinari's old-age financial plans for the first time.

'I have a question for you, Maho, seeing as you used to

work at a securities company,' said Kinari. 'With iDeCo, you can choose where to invest the money, right? Currently I have half in cash and savings, a quarter in an indexed investment fund linked to TOPIX, and a quarter in an overseas indexed stock investment fund. What do you think about that mix? I'm wondering if it might be better to increase the investment ratio. I could switch if I find a better investment trust.'

What on earth is she talking about? Indexed? Doesn't index mean list in English? And what are topics? Yasuo had no clue. It all sounded like mumbo jumbo to him, but he assumed their discussion had some rhyme and reason to it.

'Low-fee index funds are best for long-term investment, I believe. I strongly recommend choosing one with low fees, and making it compound interest.'

'I'm already doing that.'

'Exactly what I'd expect from you, Kinari!'

The two women cheered and high-fived like baseball players. Yasuo was puzzled. *What's compound interest? How can they get so excited over it?*

'But I don't know about the ratio. I would think that at your age, Kinari, you would be okay putting a higher percentage into investment trusts, but in this age of self-responsibility that's not something I could decide for you. You still have over thirty years until you receive your pension, don't you? If I were you, I'd probably ramp it up. It's not too late to transition to cash savings in your fifties.'

Self-responsibility. Yasuo never came across that word unless in the context of something scary. He observed that Kinari seemed more animated talking with Maho than she ever was with him. They had known each other for so long that these days they sometimes ate in silence.

What is this gobbledygook that Kinari and Maho keep throwing about? Does everybody know this stuff? Yasuo kept a cool face on the surface of it, but underneath he was feeling anxious. As he looked about, his eyes met those of Maho's husband, Taiyo, who was sitting so close to Yasuo that their elbows were almost knocking. Not that Yasuo was without sympathy for the Idos' simple lifestyle, but the five adults were seated around a table next to the tiny, narrow kitchen in the small three-room apartment. Some of the chairs had apparently been borrowed from a neighbour.

'Yasuo, if you'd like to smoke, you can go out on the balcony,' said Taiyo with a refreshing smile, coming to his rescue.

'Do you smoke, Yasuo?' Maho looked shocked, as if she'd discovered the root of all evil.

'Not really, just sometimes . . .'

'Yes, he does. He doesn't smoke in front of me, but when he goes away for work, he smokes where I won't know about it,' said Kinari with a frown.

She looked like a nagging wife in that moment to Yasuo, and on the strength of that he decided to go on the balcony with Taiyo, even though he didn't really feel like smoking.

'Sharp of you to catch on that I smoke,' he said, 'when I hardly ever do.'

'A lot of the older guys at work smoke,' Taiyo said. 'It doesn't bother me – I'm used to it.'

Yasuo could imagine Taiyo out drinking with his older colleagues, being attentive, efficiently finding seats where smoking was permitted, and proffering the ashtray. No doubt he was well-liked by all.

'I get the urge to smoke whenever I have a drink.'

They ate Maho's homemade pizza and drank the hard-to-find craft beer that Kinari had brought. The pizza was delicious, made from dough using a bread maker Maho had bought with credit card points.

'I thought firefighters didn't smoke because they have to keep in shape. And smoking in bed causes fires, too.'

'A lot of public servants smoke – it's an old-fashioned work culture. But hey, sorry about in there. Maho talking her head off.'

This apology, too, came across as a kind of bragging in Yasuo's ears. 'Hey, no hard feelings,' he said. 'I'm glad you invited us. I learned all kinds of stuff listening to them. Kinari seems to be enjoying herself, more than she does with me, anyway.'

'Maho's usually on her own with Saho. She likes having the chance to talk with adults. Especially someone she hits it off with so well as Kinari.'

'I guess it must be tough raising a kid,' Yasuo mumbled, as if this was a world completely unrelated to him. He did not understand why people had children. Earlier, he had been playing with Saho on his lap until she went down for her nap. She had approached him quite naturally and asked to be held. The other adults teased Yasuo about this: 'Children can tell, you know.' Even overseas, Yasuo had often had the experience of children and animals coming up to him. It wasn't that he disliked children – he simply did not want them himself.

Naturally, he had no desire to deny other people the right to have children and did not criticise. But in his opinion, they were expensive, time-consuming and a lot of work. You could expend immense amounts of time and effort on them, and still have no guarantee they would turn out all right. Instead of being cared for in your old age, you might even end up being beaten to death with a metal bat. As he saw it, the comparative return on costs was low. Children basically were bad cost-performance. The worst kind of cost-effectiveness, in fact. It was a mystery to Yasuo how the economically-minded Maho could be on board with the ultimately low cost-performance of a child.

The fact that Yasuo even thought this, went some way towards explaining why he was still single. Even he himself thought that he was a cold fish. Inexplicably, however, people often took him to be the opposite.

'It was all gibberish to me,' said Yasuo.

'To be honest, I didn't understand it either.'

'What? You too, Taiyo?'

'Maho takes care of all our money and investments.' He smiled again, showing his white teeth.

Yasuo was frankly amazed. *How can he live like that,* he thought, *handing over all the money he earns to his wife, without complaint or concern?* Maybe this was a necessary condition of being equipped to have a family and raise children. That, too, was a special ability.

'I like it that way,' Taiyo continued. 'Things work better with a tough, sensible woman in charge to keep the house running. My parents are like that.'

Yasuo could see his point, and yes, it was one way of looking at it. He, too, did not dislike strong women. Until now, Kinari had been pouring that capability not into a marriage, but into sticking it out alone while Yasuo flitted about overseas and to far-flung parts of Japan. But now, he was frankly impressed with Taiyo's argument. Marriage might be better than he thought.

'I'm learning a lot from talking with you, Taiyo.' These days he hardly ever talked with anyone who had followed a regular path in life, finding a job and getting married.

'I doubt it. There's nothing I could teach someone like you, Yasuo,' said Taiyo, self-deprecatingly.

'You're such a good-looking guy, you could be a poster boy for the fire department.'

'I already was, once. After three years on the job, I was asked to model for the recruiting posters. It took up a whole day of one of my days off, and I never received a single yen in payment. Then I had to put up with everyone laughing and making jokes. It was the pits.'

He didn't even brag about this. What a perfect dad.

Kinari was in a good mood on the way home. 'Aren't Maho and Taiyo a lovely couple? I wasn't sure what to expect since they're not the kind of people we usually see, but Maho is so financially aware – I'd like to interview her. Maybe I can propose an article for a magazine,' she finished, musing aloud.

'I bet they're saying the same as us.'

'Do you think? I hope so,' Kinari responded, without sarcasm.

Whoa, what's up with her? Yasuo wondered. Kinari's habitual sardonic and occasionally harsh evaluations of other people, was something he liked about her.

'Don't you want us to have children, too?' she said.

Yasuo didn't know what to say. *Why do women want to have children with me? Could there be anybody more unsuited to having kids than me?* This year he would be turning forty, and it was not the first, or even second time that he had received such a proposal. In fact he had been asked it more times than he could count on two hands, including light-hearted suggestions while still a student, and others in the heat of the moment in bed.

When he remained silent, Kinari started to explain why she thought Yasuo would be a suitable father for her child. He was, she told him, relatively well-educated, relatively manly and a relatively kind person.

She must have been thinking about it for a while, Yasuo realised, and this outpouring triggered by their visit to the Idos'. He was all too painfully aware of the position she was in. Which is why he was not up to the task of denying her. But as a matter of practical concern, how could he – a man with no regular job, no dreams for the future and interested only in living an easy life – have children?

'I don't even pay my pension contributions and my health insurance has lapsed.' Yasuo didn't know if that was an answer, but he said it anyway.

'I know.'

Aha, so she did know. 'And of course, I have no savings.'

'I know that too.'

'I don't know how long I can keep living in my grandmother's house.'

The only reason Yasuo could survive was because he didn't have to pay rent. But the house belonged to a relative and he was merely the caretaker. He could be evicted at any time and have no right to complain.

'I didn't know that.' Still, Kinari did not sound too depressed about it.

'Given all that, is it really a good idea?'

Yasuo meant to imply it wasn't, but Kinari's answer was a resounding 'Yes, it is! I'll be the breadwinner, and you can live with me. We can move to a bigger place since a portion of the rent is a business expense.'

'No, I can't.'

'Try looking at it another way. If we can deal with everything, it will be fine.'

'Deal with what?'

'The obstacles you just mentioned. You pay into the pension fund from now on – it's possible to make back payments for two years, you know – and you also join my health insurance as a family member. You can become a house husband.'

'Hmm.' Yasuo had no answer to this.

That day after arriving home, alone, he checked the updates of his close on ten thousand friends on Facebook. Upon finding one who was currently working the saury fishing season, he sent a message asking about the chances of him finding work there. He got the friend to set it up immediately, then fled Tokyo. He had not seen Kinari since.

*

Yasuo had graduated from university in the 2000s, at a time when the market for jobseekers was at its worst. The number of job openings had dropped to the same number of jobseekers, and even offers for new graduates had fallen. For every hundred graduates there were only ninety positions available.

At university he had floated through life as lightly as he did now, the difference being that back then he had thought it would only be temporary, until he graduated. Even Yasuo hadn't always been this way. Despite constantly hearing that the economy was in trouble, he had somehow underestimated the impact of this, and had counted on there being at least one or two companies that he could get a toehold in upon graduation. In retrospect, he saw that vanity about his university's standing had led him to overestimate his prospects.

His grades were terrible because of his constant part-time work and travels. When it came to the job-hunting season, he'd applied to lots of publishing companies, with little preparation, and failed to find a position at any of them. As graduation approached, eventually he decided in desperation to apply anywhere, and was accepted for a sales position at a real estate company. On his first day at work, in the branch office he had been assigned to near the train line in a well-heeled part of Tokyo, he was berated by a senior member of staff for not serving tea properly. Then, after being made to stand – with no instruction or guidance whatsoever – in a sandwich board outside the station to advertise the tall narrow houses for small plots of land known in Japan as 'pencil houses', he simply quit. Leaning the sandwich board against a guard rail at the station, he walked off and never even went back to the office. Later, he sent a letter of resignation by mail and changed his cell phone number.

Yasuo never regretted it, for it later became known that this very same company was notorious for exploiting their workers, when a new employee committed suicide. Deep down, however, he was afraid that the outcome would have been the same no matter where he went. When Yasuo was born, his father had chosen characters for his name that represented his hope for this second son to have a safe, secure and peaceful life, even if he never did anything great or important.

Yasuo had the feeling that wish might have backfired. A girlfriend he met through one of his part-time jobs used to make joking puns about his name, calling him Lightweight Yasuo. She left him when he refused to marry her, with the mocking words, *'You really are insignificant, aren't you? With a name like Yasuo, you can only live an insignificant life.'* She went on to marry the scion of a certain IT company, live in an exclusive Roppongi Hills apartment and have two children. Even now, she still sends Yasuo a lavish New Year's card every year, as if to taunt him.

Yasuo, on the other hand, was not convinced that an insignificant life was such a bad thing. He earned an average of ¥250,000 a month from seasonal work, or ¥300,000 at most. Depending on the job, meals and dormitory accommodation were provided, so his living expenses were not high. In two or three months he could earn a respectable amount that he then used to go on a trip somewhere, or back to the house in Jujo, according to his whim.

At home, he mostly cooked for himself every day. He grew his own vegetables, and bought fish in bulk when it was cheap, which he then dried himself. If he didn't have any supply of rice, which he sometimes received after working on farms, he would buy it, along with bread crusts from the bakery for ¥30 a bag. With books to be borrowed for free from the library, he was able to lead, on a small scale, the kind of life evoked in the old Japanese proverb 'work in the fields on fine days and read when it rains'. Or perhaps that of 'an educated idler', as another proverb might have it. Although Yasuo thought he might not be as educated as all that.

It was true, as he had previously told Kotoko, that he could live on ¥1 million a year. Less even, in fact. This was why he was apt to quit a job as soon as he had earned a sizeable sum of money.

Yasuo was one of life's dropouts. But he was happy, and of the mind that he was probably beyond going back to an ordinary way of life any more.

'I hear you're out of Tokyo again?' said Kotoko when she rang the next day, which was unusual for her. Yasuo was relaxing in the dormitory after a bath at the end of the working day. 'You shouldn't be doing that.'

'I'm sorry,' he blurted immediately, as if Kotoko knew what he had been up to the previous day, but then realised there was no way she could know.

Why did I say that? And how does Kotoko know I'm not in Tokyo in the first place? Are she and Kinari in contact? Kinari had got on so well with both Maho and Kotoko, maybe she had gone and blabbed to Kotoko. *I proposed to Yasuo, but instead of giving an answer he took off without a word,* or something like that. Yasuo was even more exasperated. He hated it when women ganged up on him. *Teacher, Yasuo made Kinari cry. He's a bad boy!* It was so childish. Like a class meeting. Maho was the class president and Kotoko the form teacher.

He was disappointed in Kotoko, whom he'd always thought of as a cool old lady, and straightforward about things.

'You should have told me – how can I water the garden?'

'Excuse me?' He was taken by surprise, not having anticipated an offensive from this direction. Then he realised he had been making assumptions. Kotoko would never poke her nose into someone else's business needlessly, even if asked for advice.

'It may be autumn, but the weather is still hot, you know. I took over some Chinese cabbage and snow-pea seeds to give you for autumn planting, but you weren't there. It was a bit of a surprise to see the flowers in the garden looking sad. I felt sorry for them, so I gave them a quick sprinkle.'

'Thank you very much.'

'Plants don't have legs, you know. They have no choice about where they're put, however hard or painful it may be. They are there at the convenience of the humans who plant them. You have to be responsible.'

Kotoko could get quite vehement when it came to flowers and vegetables. It was sweet. Yasuo hadn't given his garden a thought since fleeing Tokyo. But he'd always run from anything the slightest bit awkward. There was no way someone like him should have children – he couldn't even look after plants.

'I asked Kinari, but she said you'd gone off and she didn't know where you were.'

Aha, so she did know.

'Did something happen?'

Yasuo was ready to be defiant if she tried to meddle; instead he was touched by her unexpectedly gentle tone. 'Did Kinari say anything?'

'No. Kinari's not the sort to go telling tales. I wouldn't think of asking her either – it's young people's business. But it's not like you to leave without a word of goodbye.'

It was true, he'd never done anything like this since meeting Kotoko.

'Kinari and I have a ... situation,' Yasuo said. He couldn't very well go into the details. There was Kinari to consider as well.

'Is that so?'

'Er, yeah.'

'Come home for a bit.'

'I can't leave now, I only just started here, and had to beg to get this job in the first place.'

'Don't you get time off?'

'Yes, I do.'

'Then just take a day off. You need to decide where to sow those Chinese cabbage, and potherb mustard and snow-pea seeds. I also got hold of some brown mustard seeds. They taste slightly hot but are delicious. I'll give you some of that, too.'

Yasuo was grateful. Nonetheless ...

'Shouldn't you have a proper chat with Kinari?'

'Uh, but ...'

'If you don't plant those seeds now, there won't be anything to put in the hotpot when winter comes. You haven't planted your Chinese cabbage yet this year, have you?'

Yasuo's head was almost exploding with the incessant talk of vegetables. Then it occurred to him: *But that's why I like Kotoko. She enjoys life, sowing her Chinese cabbage in autumn, carefully tending it for a couple of months and looking forward to eating it in a nice hotpot.* His own grandmother had done the same. Old people had a way of saying things that sometimes stuck in the mind and took you by surprise. *If I go back now to plant the Chinese cabbage, as Kotoko suggests, and talk with Kinari while I'm there, could I make a better go of things?*

'Won't you come back?'

'I'll see if I can get a day off.' It was also true that he found himself wanting to go home a bit. Not only because of what Kotoko had said – Yasuo was thinking of what he had done last night.

'Chinese cabbage always grows bigger than you think, so make sure to leave lots of space.'

'But it only grows to thirty centimetres in diameter at most, doesn't it?'

'You're thinking of the Chinese cabbage that you see in shops. The leaves spread wide open like a flower as it grows at first, then close up like a bulb to form a head. You need a good forty centimetres between the roots.'

Though Yasuo had had repeated messages from Kotoko telling him to hurry up and plant his Chinese cabbage because the seeds required a high germination temperature, when he arrived he found her waiting with seedlings she had already grown from seed. Yasuo planted the Chinese cabbage seedlings at the far end of his one-and-a-half-square-metre vegetable patch, in a corner of the garden, and sowed mizuna and mustard green seeds in front. He also put stakes for snow pea, green pea and snap pea seedlings in the fifty-centimetre gap between the house and the fence along the western side of the house. Before meeting Kotoko he had not made use of this dead space, but at her recommendation had begun planting it with cucumbers and bitter gourd in summer, and vine vegetables such as peas in the winter. They did well there, despite receiving only the western sunlight.

'There's nothing like fresh-picked green peas. They taste so sweet; once you use them to cook your own rice and beans, you'll never eat the ready-made version again.'

'I can't eat all this stuff I've planted. I might not be at home, either.'

Kotoko remained silent. Her expression was tense.

'I'm sorry.' Yasuo knew from experience that when a woman's face stiffened like this, it was better to apologise, even if he didn't know what for.

'Don't you worry. I'll eat them. I can give some to the neighbours, too.' Kotoko smiled, and a large dimple appeared in her right cheek. *I bet fifty years ago men were charmed by that look,* thought Yasuo. Even now it had charm, and he was incapable of saying no to her.

'Did you contact Kinari?'

'No.'

'I knew it.'

'I thought you didn't meddle in young people's affairs.'

'I'm not meddling, I just think it's a shame.'

At that moment, they heard the rattling of the front door as it slid open, and a voice called out hello. Kinari's voice.

'What did you just say?' Yasuo glared at her.

'I wanted to consult Kinari about something, that's all,' said Kotoko breezily. 'Kinari, we're out here, in the garden,' she called.

Kinari walked through the house and poked her head in from outside the enclosed porch. 'I brought cake, shall I make tea?' She smiled as if nothing had happened.

'Yes please,' Kotoko replied, 'but I'll only have tea. I'm going out soon.'

Yasuo watched Kinari disappear into the kitchen, then scowled at Kotoko again.

'Leaving so soon, are you, now you've stirred things up?' he said.

'It's true, I do have to go to the hospital.'

He could hardly be angry at that. 'Is something wrong?'

'Not with me, my daughter-in-law is in hospital, and I'm going with the grandchildren to visit. A family gathering after so long and it's in a hospital.' Kotoko sounded a little sad.

Kinari and Yasuo sat across from each other at the kitchen table, drinking tea.

'Will you really not be able to continue living here?' Kinari said, looking around.

It's like she doesn't remember last time we met, thought Yasuo. 'Someday. It doesn't belong to me,' he said.

'But didn't you say your grandmother wrote that she was leaving it to you?' Yasuo had continued to visit his grandmother until the end, and she had indeed left a will saying that she wanted to leave the house to him. The truth was, however, that he hadn't been as attentive to his grandmother as it might sound. It was difficult for a job-hopper like Yasuo to go back home and live with his parents intermittently, and so he had stayed with his grandmother in between overseas trips and casual jobs in remote places. He was well aware that he was the one being looked after, never the other way round.

'It wasn't a legally binding will, and even if it was, my relatives also had rights to it, too, so it would've had to be shared.'

Yasuo had heard about what could happen in such situations from another seasonal worker who was taking the bar exam and knew about such things. It convinced him that it would be easier to give up his rights to the house, rather than get caught up in family squabbles over property. Fortunately, his relatives allowed him to continue living there for now.

'I wish I had the money to buy it. Either way, my relatives will have to sell it and divide the money up sometime.'

There was bound to be trouble when that happened, so for now they were holding off, letting things slide for the time being. Not unlike Kinari and himself. Talking about minor things, and putting off discussion of the really important stuff.

'So, what are you going to do?'

Perhaps Kinari was not as willing to procrastinate as Yasuo thought.

'Yeah, that is the question . . .'

'Come and live with me. Setting aside what I said before, I don't want to break up with you.'

'I appreciate it, but are you really fine with that?'

'It's okay. Just don't go off again without telling me. I won't ask anything of you, except that – don't disappear on me.'

Yasuo could have said sure, and continued as though nothing had happened, but he wasn't quite that bad a person.

'I did a lot of thinking, but I just can't bring myself to say yes to having kids.' He wanted to make that much clear at least.

'Why not?'

'It's the one thing I don't think I can do. Not only financially, but also because of my personality. I'm not tolerant, or patient, or responsible enough. I lack all those qualities. And I just don't have the courage.'

Kinari was silent for a moment. 'I understand.'

'I wanted to say, if you find a better man, it's okay to leave me.'

'Is that what you want?' Kinari laughed sadly.

'It can't be helped.'

'You really are awful.'

I guess I am, thought Yasuo. 'But I'll quit this current job and come back.'

'What? You'd do that?'

'I'll hang around for a while. I gave you a hard time, and want to make things good between us. I also have Chinese cabbage to grow.'

Kinari laughed again, even more wistfully this time. 'You really are a terrible person. A terrible person.' She looked up at Yasuo through upturned eyes, and scowled at him briefly. 'I end up not even being angry with you.'

And with this exchange the quarrel with Kinari was smoothed over, as usual.

What happened next, however, came as a bolt from the blue. Yasuo was awoken by a voice.

'Can I have some water?'

For a moment he didn't know where he was.

'Komori-san.'

He opened one eye. Dazzling autumn light filtered in. He opened the other eye and his vision came into focus.

'You?' he said stupidly.

He had fallen asleep while reading on the enclosed porch, after a morning spent working in the vegetable patch.

'Yes, me.'

Before him was Rena. Rena, whose name he knew how to pronounce but still not how to write. In her arms she held the tortoiseshell cat that Yasuo was taking care of for his neighbour while she was away overseas. Kodama was its name. This neighbour had refused Yasuo's own request to water his garden when he was away, but had no compunction about leaving her cat with him when she went off. He thought that unfair. But he couldn't refuse because Kodama was such a sweet, timid cat, and no trouble at all, so he didn't mind too much.

'What are you doing here?'

Kodama squirmed in Rena's arms. Rena held tight, resisting letting her go. The sight of her muscular fingers digging into Kodama gave Yasuo a bad feeling.

'First of all, I'd like a glass of water, please.'

'Would you mind letting the cat go?'

'What?'

'The cat. It doesn't like that.'

Rena released it and Kodama scurried off.

Yasuo slowly rose to his feet, scratching his sides, and headed for the kitchen. He took mineral water from the refrigerator and poured it into a glass. As he watched the water flow, his head cleared and the sense of foreboding deepened. *Uh-oh. I don't know what she's up to but I have a bad feeling about this. Why is she here? I didn't even give her my phone number or contact information.* Feigning calm, he carried the water out to Rena. She took it without a word of thanks, and sat down on the edge of the porch to drink, baring her white throat as she leaned back.

'What's going on?' Yasuo asked, before she had finished.

'What do you mean?' she replied, in a provocatively collected manner.

'How'd you get my address?'

'I got someone at the office to tell me. They showed me your CV.'

'How'd you manage that?' Weren't there supposed to be strict rules about divulging personal information? But Rena was so popular with all the guys, Yasuo could easily imagine it being a pushover for her to wangle his details out of someone.

'I said I was pregnant with your child and they gave it to me.'

Hahaha, Yasuo laughed automatically. He didn't mind a joke.

'I bet that guy was jealous.' Still, why turn up here? Yasuo was puzzled. Then he noticed: Rena was not smiling. 'You're joking, right?'

'What would you say if I told you I wasn't?'

'Are you serious?'

'I wouldn't joke about that.'

Yasuo gulped. 'I . . . I don't . . .' I don't want kids, he was about to say, then backed down. 'Well . . . let's talk.'

'Yes, let's.' Rena picked up the travelling bag at her feet, and stepped firmly up into the house. 'That's why I'm here.'

She wore ballet shoes and ankle socks. *Low heels because she's pregnant? Socks to keep from getting cold?* Yasuo observed, feeling oddly dispassionate.

'We only did it once, right,' he blurted.

'Yeees.' Rena drew the word out slowly.

Whether this was an answer to his question, or an automatic reply, Yasuo didn't know, but already her voice was sounding from deep inside the house.

Before anything else there was one thing Yasuo had to do. He waited for Kinari in a coffee shop in the Jujo shopping district.

'Why the hurry, Yasuo? I'll be seeing you tonight.'

They had planned a hotpot dinner at Yasuo's place that evening. He had thinned out the seedlings in his vegetable patch, reaping mizuna for the hotpot and mustard greens for a salad. Kinari was going to bring thin-sliced pork for the hotpot.

'I just splashed out on some of that Berkshire pork loin from Kagoshima at the Sakai butcher shop. Apparently the fat is very sweet and tasty,' she told him, looking pleased as she held up a package for him to see.

'Actually . . .' he said, and faltered. Bitter saliva rose in his throat.

'What's wrong?' Kinari was catching on that something had happened to Yasuo. 'You don't look so good,' she said.

'I just want to say up front that I only did it once.'

'What?'

'Please remember that, and hear me out.'

'Did what, only once?'

Yasuo swallowed his spit. 'Did it. That is to say . . .' Yeah, *that*.

Yasuo really had only done it that one time, soon after his arrival in the fishing port. It had been completely unintended, a spur-of-the-moment thing, and he had managed to deflect Rena every time she approached him again afterwards. He had returned to Tokyo for Kinari's sake, of course, but the fact that Rena was becoming a nuisance also had something to do with it. If he was being honest with himself.

'There's a woman in my house right now.'

'A woman?' Kinari's expression hardened.

'A girl I met while I was working the saury catch.'

'This year? Where you were until recently?' Kinari was gradually catching on. The expression on her face turning from concern to anger. 'Are you saying you did it once with that girl?'

'Yes.'

'Idiot!' She reached over and smacked Yasuo on the head.

'I'm sorry.'

If only that was all. If only. Bad as it was.

'And that girl has turned up at your house?'

'Yeah, that's what it looks like.'

'You utter fool!'

Yasuo waited as Kinari reeled through a list of rebukes: why did you give her your address; why did you lead her on so much she would follow you home; you're being taken advantage of, and so on. He didn't pay too much heed as he knew this was just a warm-up, to what would be coming next. But the list was getting too long. 'Will you calm down and listen.' Yasuo brought Kinari up short.

'Why?'

'That's not all.'

Kinari closed her mouth. Staring at him, reproachfully.

'The fact is . . . she says she's pregnant.'

'Nooo!'

Yasuo knew he would never forget the shock and sorrow in Kinari's voice.

'She says she's pregnant. I talked with her a bit and she's not interested in an abortion. I told her I'm really sorry but I don't want a child, I don't have any feelings for her and it wouldn't end well if we married. I think she understands now. I asked her to please think a bit more carefully before deciding anything.'

Kinari remained silent, tears sliding down her face.

'But right now that girl . . . Rena's her name,' and I still don't know how to write that let alone what her family name is, 'is saying that she wants to have the baby, get married and raise it together in that house.'

Kinari slumped on her left elbow in despair, covering one eye with the palm of her hand. Her shoulders began shaking. She could not speak.

'I'll keep trying to get through to her. I know almost nothing about her, anyway. So . . .'

'I wondered when this would happen,' Kinari croaked, as if dragging out the words.

'What?'

'I was always worried this might happen one day.'

'You were?' *Why didn't you warn me?* Yasuo screamed in his head.

'Because you, my dear, are a drifter. You don't take things seriously.'

In all their long relationship, it was the first time Kinari had ever called him my dear.

'I don't know what to do any more,' she said, pulling a handkerchief from her bag to wipe her face. But she covered her face with both hands as soon as she finished, as once again tears began spilling over.

'*I* wanted to marry you. *I* wanted a child with you, too. I've always dreamed of it.'

In jagged sentences, Kinari asked about Rena. How old was she, what did she look like, what university did she go to, where did her parents live, what did they do, and so on. Yasuo did his best to answer her questions, but he knew almost nothing about Rena. Every time he spoke, Kinari knocked him on the head and shed more tears.

'Why her? Why not me?' she wailed loudly. 'I always dreamed of being with you in old age. Living in a big flat with the mortgage paid off, not especially wealthy but still able to travel sometimes, the kids independent, and you by my side. I'm not dreaming too big, am I? Why can't my dream come true?'

Kinari's cries echoed through the coffee shop. By now, the other customers were aware of the unfolding scene and a hush had fallen. Some had looked over curiously at first, but now no one was looking and one or two people departed awkwardly.

'Maybe we were never fated to be together after all,' Kinari said in a low voice, almost as if to herself. She rose to her feet unsteadily. 'A wedding gift,' she said with a painful smile, glancing at the package of pork still on the table, and left.

'So in the end she wasn't pregnant after all?'

'No.'

A week later, Yasuo was sitting opposite Kotoko eating hotpot. The meat was the same pork which Kinari had given Yasuo that day. Understandably, he had not been in any mood for eating it with Rena, and had put it straight into the freezer.

The pregnancy fiasco had been resolved within the space of a few days. It was a simple matter; Rena's period had started and she left.

'Why didn't you check properly before telling Kinari? You can easily get one of those things from the chemist. And it would have been better to see a doctor, too.'

'Men don't know about that kind of thing. Besides, I've always avoided anything to do with marriage and pregnancy, so I probably didn't have all the information. Whenever I see TV commercials and stuff, my brain just blocks it out.'

'Maybe the pregnancy story was a lie from the beginning.'

'What?'

'She might have been saying it to test you. Then gave up when you wouldn't go along with it.'

Yasuo hadn't realised Rena would turn out to be so tenacious.

'Did you contact Kinari?'

'I tried.'

The potherb mustard seedlings were tender and delicious. Ordinarily Yasuo could have eaten any amount of them, lightly dunked in the simmering water then wrapped in a piece of the Berkshire pork and flavoured with some of Kotoko's homemade ponzu citrus dipping sauce. Today, however, he had no appetite. Even though it was the first decent meal he had eaten since Rena arrived at his house.

'I sent Kinari a LINE message to tell her Rena wasn't pregnant.'

'You should be eating this with Kinari, not me,' Kotoko said, pointing to the plate of pork.

'She read the message, but I didn't get an answer.'

'You sent one message and that's it?'

'Yes.'

'You have to keep trying.'

'I'm tired too, after this past week, I don't have the energy.'

'You really are the limit. How can you be so selfish as to think of Kinari in that way? I didn't think you were that kind of person.'

Yasuo had often heard this same sentiment expressed by other people: I didn't think you were that kind of person.

I thought you were better than that. He wished people wouldn't take it on themselves to expect something from him and then be disappointed.

'But don't you think she might be a little relieved?'

'Of course she is, nonetheless ... She's probably kicking herself for being so foolish. Or I don't know, maybe she's fed up with being at your mercy.'

Kotoko was being unsympathetic today.

'I see what you mean.'

'In fact, after hearing your story just now, I don't think I like you as much any more.'

'I'm sorry.' Yasuo hung his head dejectedly.

'Even if she wasn't pregnant, the fact remains that you cheated on Kinari.'

'True. But it was only once.'

Abruptly, Kotoko pulled back her chopsticks from the hotpot.

'I've lost my appetite.'

'I'm sorry.'

'You should be saying that to Kinari, not me.'

Steam rose from the bubbling hotpot, that neither was dipping their chopsticks into any more.

'What should I do?'

'Simple. Just keep saying sorry. Apologise, apologise, apologise.' Kotoko peered into his face. 'You do love Kinari, don't you?'

'Of course I do.'

Yasuo stared at the surface of the pot. 'All this got me thinking ... While she was here, Rena that is ... I was wishing it was Kinari. If I was going to have a kid, at least why couldn't it be with Kinari? How did this happen? Maybe I could accept having a kid, after all.'

'So now you think you might want to marry Kinari. Why don't you just say so?'

'Well, yes, but would it really work in practice if we married? The problem hasn't really been solved and things haven't changed, so I don't know what to say to Kinari.'

'But you had that thought, didn't you, that you'd like to have a child with her? That's a true feeling, I believe.'

'I guess so, but thinking about it . . .'

'Thinking about what? Why can't you have children?'

'Err . . . but I have to think about cost-effectiveness.'

'Cost-effectiveness? If you let cost-effectiveness come into it you will absolutely never be able to have children. Children and marriage are nothing but logic-defying. Tell me, where is the cost-effectiveness in your current way of life? All you do is travel and take casual jobs. Is that how you'll live until you die? What's so marvellous about that? What in heaven's name does travelling do for you?'

'You could say I want to improve myself.'

'Improve yourself? If you turned it into writing an article or book like Kinari, I might understand, but what use do *you* make of your improved self?'

Kotoko was not usually this sarcastic.

I know, thought Yasuo. *I don't need Kotoko to tell me that. It's why I've been running all this time, never thinking deeply about my life before.* Having been so roundly scolded, however, Yasuo could not remain silent. 'Do I have to produce something to have a result? If I can improve my mind, that's enough of a result for me. To live a life that satisfies me.'

'Satisfies you? Fine, you keep living in this house by yourself and be satisfied.' Kotoko stood up, grabbed her bag and stalked off to the front door.

Yasuo hurried after her. *She must really be angry,* he thought.

'Cost-effectiveness? Hahaha. If cost-effectiveness is so important to you, why don't you die now. No need to eat, spend money on clothes or fix up the house – you won't need any money. That would be the ultimate cost-effectiveness, don't you think? You wouldn't have to bother working, either,' Kotoko spat as she walked. 'If your parents had been thinking about cost-effectiveness, you wouldn't be on this earth in the first place.' Kotoko put on her shoes at the front entrance and turned to look back. 'Life is irrational. What's the point of economising if not for those irrational things? For the economy? Economising is what you do, once you accept life. And life is not about cost-effectiveness. Otherwise the only conclusion to draw is that it's better for an old person like me to be dead.'

'I'm sorry, I didn't mean that.' Yasuo stepped outside onto the ground barefoot, and caught at Kotoko's coat, as if he didn't want to let her leave. 'I was wrong. I truly am sorry. Please don't go.'

'You really are a nincompoop!' She smacked him on the head. Quite hard. 'That's the first time I ever hit somebody else's child.' Kotoko exhaled loudly in exasperation. 'I might've gone too far. I'm sorry.'

'But what am I going to do? About Kinari, too?'

'Take her some flowers and sweets, and tell her your feelings honestly. Then get down on your knees.'

'And if she still won't forgive me?'

'Flowers, sweets, get down on your knees and beg. When you've begged once, do it again. Then propose to her.'

'What?'

'You've already made up your mind, haven't you?'

Have I? Yasuo wondered. *Have I really made up my mind?* Still with Kotoko's lapel in his hand, he hung his head.

'I'll say it once more. Make sure you hang on to Kinari like you're doing to me now. Don't let go.' Kotoko pointed to Yasuo's hands clutching at her coat. 'Deplorable as you are, there's something in you that gives a woman cause to hope there might be hidden depths of goodness and kindness. That's why they stay around. Even I can't help but think that there really is something more to you, that the real you is different. It's a dirty trick.'

It was true. People's first impressions of Yasuo were of a friendly, likeable guy, but then they would become angry with him when those expectations were betrayed.

'I'm not saying you have to get married or have children. But if you love Kinari and don't want to let her go, you need to talk and find a mutual compromise. The most important thing to remember is that any relationship where only one person is making sacrifices will never get off the ground.'

'I understand.' But Yasuo couldn't help wondering if he was capable of that.

*

He was standing in front of Kinari's block of flats when she arrived back. Of course she did not return his smile. This was the third day he had gone to her flat. The lobby was on auto-lock so he could not enter, and could only push his sweet offerings into the post box. Yesterday he had brought chocolate croissants and the day before that chestnut-bean jelly from Minatoya where Kotoko worked.

So far, this had not elicited any response from Kinari, and so today Yasuo had decided to wait for her. That way he would have a better chance of catching her coming or going at some point. Yasuo had all the time in the world.

He arrived outside the building at midday. Although it was the end of September the sun was still hot, but he had come prepared with a bamboo peasant hat, which he had bought in Vietnam a long time ago, a bottle of water, a folding chair and a paperback copy of *Yokoshigure* (Wind-Driven Rain) by Saiichi Maruya to pass the time. Kinari lived in a secluded residential area of Akabane, where there were few passers-by. He attracted the occasional look of suspicion but was thankful not to be reported. Perhaps the chair made him look like someone conducting a traffic survey. Kinari arrived home around eight at night, when Yasuo had been waiting for eight whole hours.

'Kinari!' he yelled as she went to enter the front door after only a quick glance at him.

'Please, will you at least accept this?'

Today, at Kotoko's advice, he had brought a small bouquet of wilted flowers, which he had bought for ¥500 from a florist in the shopping mall.

Unable to think of what other sweet treat he could bring, he had also brought a loaf of bread from a popular bakery in the mall, which always had long queues outside it.

'How long have you been here?' Kinari said, punching in the numbers for the door lock.

'Since noon.'

'All this time?'

'Yeah.'

'Idiot.' She looked down at the bread. 'I can't eat that much.'

'You can throw the leftovers away.'

'I'm not the kind of person who can throw away food.'

At this, Yasuo put down everything in his hands, and got down on his hands and knees. His head scraped the ground. 'I'm so terribly sorry. I don't expect you to forgive me, but I just wanted to tell you how I feel.'

He heard Kinari taking deep breaths.

'In any case, I'm sorry. I was really stupid.'

When no reply came, Yasuo raised his head in trepidation. Kinari merely looked sorrowful. Quickly, Yasuo bowed his head again. 'I'm so sorry.'

'Sorry? Screw you!'

Yasuo felt a sharp pain in his posterior, and fell sideways. Kinari had given him a sound kick, not holding back at all. For a moment he could not breathe for the pain. He remembered that Kinari had played soccer at high school and even been selected to represent the prefecture at one time.

'Take this at least. Seeing as I bought it.' Yasuo thrust his gift at her as she was about to go inside. Kinari took it with lifeless hands, like a doll.

'I just want to say one thing.' It hurt to even speak. 'While that girl was around, the whole time I was wishing it was you, and thinking, if I'm going to have a child, why can't it be with Kinari.'

Kinari looked down at him. She did not speak.

'I still can't think about marriage, but if I did, it would be with you. Can we talk again?'

Yasuo felt himself smacked around the head with the bouquet of flowers. Tiny blossoms fell to the ground.

'Don't say things like that!'

'But, but . . . can I email, or ring?'

Kinari hesitated. 'I don't know,' she said, and stalked off into the building.

Yasuo waited until she had disappeared from sight, then slowly stood up. Nothing seemed to be broken – he simply hurt all over. He picked up the folding chair.

She didn't say I couldn't email. I guess that means it's okay to continue.

He would come again tomorrow. He did not have much, but he had time. Yasuo had always tried to travel lightly through life, but for the first time he felt attached to someone.

How can I tell her this?

He walked off, dragging the aluminium chair behind him.

5

The Economics of Divorce in Middle Age

The house felt cold when Tomoko Mikuriya returned home after a long absence. It smelled stuffy, not in a bad way, just a distinct odour that she had never noticed before. *Is this the smell of my house?* she thought. Tomoko felt disorientated, but told herself it was only natural that things should seem strange after ten days in hospital.

'I'm home,' she said out loud, knowing there would be no response. It was comforting to simply say the words. She went into the living room and sat down on the sofa. Her abdomen gave a faint uncomfortable twinge.

Twenty-three years ago, Tomoko and her husband had taken out a thirty-year loan to build this house. They still had a little way to go before it was fully repaid, but the house belonged to them. It was their home.

The cost of maintaining a free-standing house had been more than they anticipated, as the exterior required repainting every five years and a roof inspection at the same time. Out the front, in a space hardly large enough to swing a mouse, let alone a cat, Tomoko had planted ivy at the suggestion of her mother-in-law, who was something of an expert in gardening, and recommended it as easy to look after. Naturally, Tomoko had been diligent with housework and cleaning, and was confident that they had expended reasonable money and effort on the house. In spite of which, it felt uninviting and in a terrible mess.

Well, perhaps not *that* much of a mess, since she usually kept it orderly and tidy, but there was a fine layer of dust over everything. Had her mother-in-law really been in a few times as promised to do the cleaning? Tomoko was certain her husband had not run the vacuum cleaner over the carpet once, or even given the floor a going-over with cleaning wipes. The lack of care was all the more noticeable for having come directly from a hospital, where there was not a speck of dust in sight. Her irritation mounted. She wanted to clean. But it was still only ten days since her operation, and she had been instructed not to exercise for a month.

'Ask your husband to do everything for you once you get home,' the head nurse of the gynaecology department had said at her discharge briefing. 'He'll never be as attentive as now. Make the most of it and rely on him for everything. He'll be wanting to do all he can for his wife.' She laughed slyly.

The other patients, overhearing this, all laughed too. Tomoko laughed along with them, but maybe anything would have seemed amusing when in a state of anticipation at going home. *If you ask somebody to do something for you, they have to be able to do it in the first place,* she thought bitterly, lying on the sofa. *Kazuhiko is utterly incapable of doing any kind of housework. He doesn't even want to try.*

While Tomoko was in hospital, Kazuhiko had gone to his mother's house, less than a kilometre away, for dinner every night. Apparently, she had even made his bento lunchbox some days. How was it that a woman such as her mother-in-law, whose cooking and housework was faultless to a degree, had not taught her son to do these things? Or perhaps this was precisely the reason why.

Tomoko hadn't minded so much in the early days of their marriage. She was born into a generation of women of 'office ladies' when they entered the workforce during the late 1980s, in the heady days of an economic boom that came to be known as the bubble era. Her generation was derided by their elders, who claimed not to understand the thinking of this so-called new breed. *But they still made sure we had their old-fashioned values firmly drilled into us, didn't they?* Tomoko thought. They took it for granted that men did not do housework. It was a different story now for the thirty- and forty-year-olds of today, who Tomoko was slightly jealous of, but when it came to women in their twenties, like her daughters, she was beyond envy.

The bubble generation might have been mocked for having jobs handed to them on a plate, but when the bubble burst, they were the ones left to mop up the mess created by their elders.

Everyone said we were so materialistic and empty-headed, but it was dreadful what we had to put up with – the male chauvinism! Those days weren't the easy ride that everybody makes out. But at least we got to wear power suits with padded shoulders, silhouette-hugging clothes and curl our fringes, Tomoko thought sardonically.

Then, all that flattery and attention notwithstanding, once a woman married, she went into the house and there she stayed. That was the norm; a woman stayed at home and a man went out to work. And heaven forbid that husbands should do anything around the house. That, too, was a given.

Tomoko herself had grown up in such a family. But her father had been in the Self-Defense Forces, a highly trained military school graduate who was at least capable of cooking or cleaning if need arose. He didn't usually do any housework, but when Tomoko's mother had been hospitalised, Tomoko had been surprised to discover that he could make miso soup and rice.

In contrast, the men of Kazuhiko and Tomoko's generation had been coddled by their mothers. There was no complaint as long as they studied hard for university entrance exams; hence they grew up not learning how to do anything around the house. Tomoko had heard similar tales from all her friends.

Today, her daughters were supposed to have come and collected her from the hospital. But her eldest, Maho, had phoned in a fluster a week ago. 'Mum, I'm so sorry – the day you get out clashes with Saho's pre-school prep day!'

'It's fine, I'll be all right.'

'I asked Miho, so don't worry. She said she'd take the day off.'

Then Miho, too, had phoned. 'Mum, I've got a really important presentation that day. Someone switched dates on me and I can't get out of it. Grandma should be free – shall I ask her?'

'No, no, it's fine. I can get myself back.'

Tomoko didn't want her 73-year-old mother-in-law coming to get her; that was a far more stressful proposition. Besides, Kotoko had already visited Tomoko in hospital with her daughters, and made dinner for Kazuhiko. Not to mention that six months ago she'd started working part-time. *I don't want to give her any extra work,* Tomoko said to convince herself.

'I was planning to get home by myself all along. A taxi will take no time.'

'But you're not supposed to carry heavy things, are you?'

'I don't have much. If it's too heavy, I'll use a luggage delivery service.'

Tomoko noted that neither of her daughters had suggested asking their father, or said *What's Dad doing?* It had always been thus. They were used to his indifference in family matters; it was what they believed a father to be. The upshot was that Tomoko had had free rein over child-rearing, household and family finances. Kazuhiko had never once raised any objection and as long as they lived within their means, she could take whatever classes she liked, or travel, and he would not complain. He only drank and gambled in social situations, and had never once been violent. Golf was his only hobby, which he went off to play once a month with barely unconcealed excitement.

Tomoko knew his aloofness was not ill-intentioned and older women she spoke to could not understand why she was so unhappy with this state of affairs. But lying here now on the sofa in a dusty house, having just arrived home from hospital, Tomoko felt inexplicably sad.

She must have dozed off, as next thing she knew, she was awoken by a text from Kazuhiko: *We can go out for dinner or even order in. Both fine.*

Oh, right, she thought, *I'm supposed to get dinner.* Though she had known this would be the case, Tomoko wanted to sigh. Cooking was the thing her husband was least capable of. Not once in the time they had been married had he ever cooked anything. *All I've done today is come home,* she thought, *but I'm so tired.* She texted back: *Alright, let's order in.*

We could eat pizza, she decided, and stood up to go and look at the menu taped to the fridge door. It was one of the flyers that she occasionally found in the letterbox and kept in case it came in useful one day. But ever since her daughters had left home, she and Kazuhiko almost never ordered this kind of food.

While examining the colourful photos, Tomoko sighed again. *Why do I have to eat greasy food?*

Go out for dinner or even order in, Kazuhiko had written. Tomoko had suggested home delivery because the thought of leaving the house to go outside and meet her husband somewhere was too much to contemplate after having just arrived home from hospital, but pizza was the last thing she felt like eating.

Would Kazuhiko think that ordering in was *fine* if he was

the one who'd just been discharged from hospital? Had he even tried to imagine what she might be feeling?

Tomoko went to the fridge, took out some rice and carefully washed it. She always bought rice in small amounts that she transferred into plastic drink bottles and kept in the vegetable drawer. Today, she added a dash of sprouted brown rice and mixed-grain rice, which she also kept in stock and stored the same way. While waiting for the rice to cook, she made miso soup stock in a saucepan and added small pieces of diced, deep-fried tofu and leek, which she had previously made herself and frozen. Then lastly, searching through her supply of dry goods, she found a stick of dried wheat gluten to add. 'No vegetable side dish but that can't be helped. I couldn't do the shopping today,' she muttered, to no one in particular.

Before going into hospital, Tomoko had left the refrigerator virtually empty. A search of the freezer, however, turned up a packet of vacuum-packed pork marinated in miso, which had been a mid-year gift from someone. She decided to defrost this and use as another side dish. Tomoko sighed repeatedly as she worked, nonetheless impressed with herself for whipping up a meal out of nothing. She had no major pain, despite having had open abdominal surgery, but had been cautioned not to do too much standing work, and sat down at the dining table for frequent rests in the course of preparing dinner.

Ting! went her cell phone, announcing another text from Kazuhiko: *I can call my mother if it's too much.*

No, thought Tomoko, *I've made sure to keep up good relations with your mother, but if she comes over today it will be one more thing I have to think about.* Quickly, she replied: *Isn't she busy with her new job? Don't worry about it today.*

She knew that Kazuhiko was only trying his best to be considerate, but really, even after thirty years together, he was sometimes still quite ridiculous. Tomoko let out another long sigh, which was so prolonged she expelled all the air in her body.

'You cooked for me,' said Kazuhiko when he arrived home and saw the food on the table. He went and changed into something more comfortable, then turned on the TV as they began dinner. This had been the general pattern of their meals ever since the girls had left home, which Tomoko was not usually unhappy with since she believed that's what couples did. Today, however, as she ate, Tomoko could not stop thinking of all the things she wanted to say to this husband of hers, sitting in front of her and watching TV as he ate. She worried that he would take her cooking dinner as a sign that she was fine, and he could go on with his life as usual.

'I didn't feel like eating pizza or anything like that.'

'What?' Kazuhiko looked at Tomoko, still with a smile on his lips from something on the TV.

'I didn't cook because I wanted to. I did it because I was tired of hospital food and it was too much effort to go out. All I wanted was simple, normal food.'

Tomoko looked at their dinner. She had served her husband three of the five pieces of miso-marinated pork that were in the packet, and given only two to herself. The sight of it now irked her. *I didn't make this for you. I made it for me! You simply reap the benefits. I always serve you better than I do myself. Without thinking. 'Feed your husband well, because he brings in the pay cheque, so you must take better care of him than anyone else in the family . . . you must be grateful to him for bringing in money.'* Such were the voices echoing in Tomoko's mind. Who had said these things to her? Her mother? Her mother-in-law? No, nobody had ever actually said it. It had just, somehow, been ingrained in her.

'You heard what the doctor told me, didn't you? That I shouldn't do any standing work for a month or so.'

The doctor had said this to both of them the weekend before Tomoko was due to be discharged. Weekends were the only times when Kazuhiko could visit.

'That's why I suggested we ask my mother to come over.'

'If your mother came . . .' Tomoko felt too drained to continue.

'Mother offered many times to help if we needed. If you don't want her help, then ask Maho or Miho.'

They have their own lives, thought Tomoko. 'They're both busy, too, you know.'

'Then what should I do?' Kazuhiko said, which Tomoko knew was his way of trying to be kind.

'It's your fault, too, you know,' Maho had once said to Tomoko. 'You should've taught him how to cook and do housework. He's been with you longer than he ever was with Grandma. You can't just say that Grandma didn't teach him.'

Of course she takes her grandmother's side, Tomoko had thought. Both her daughters were partial to their grandmother.

Maho might well say that, but in the early days of their marriage, Kazuhiko had been even busier at work than he was now, and came home late every night. Tomoko, too, became increasingly busier once she had children, and didn't have the capacity to teach Kazuhiko housework from scratch. It was easier to do things herself than ask others. Not to mention that Kazuhiko was so clumsy and took such a long time to do anything, that Tomoko wondered if perhaps this was why her mother-in-law had also given up on teaching him to do anything around the house.

But what would happen now? With an operation imminent, Tomoko had suddenly begun to think about their old age. *Will I be cooking his meals for ever? What if I die first? Perhaps he thinks he can survive on eating out and delivery? He probably doesn't think about it at all.*

After her diagnosis, Tomoko had taken a break from the English lessons that she had been attending for years. The osechi cooking class, which she had started with her mother-in-law, was also on hold. Recently, it seemed as if all she did was see doctors and go to the hospital, so perhaps it was natural for her to feel this way.

A few days after her discharge from hospital, Tomoko's great friend Chisato Kono came to visit.

'Don't go to any trouble, I'll take care of everything,' Chisato had said, and made good on her promise by bringing a pie crammed with fruit and a bottle of ready-made green tea. Both high-end items from a Ginza department store. Apparently, tea in wine bottles is the latest thing, she informed Tomoko. Chisato always had the knack of knowing such things.

'My my, you look a lot better than I expected.'

When she heard this, Tomoko felt for the first time a real sense of actually being out of hospital. 'It's only been ten days.'

'When I saw you being wheeled out of the operating room, I got such a shock! You looked so small and helpless.'

Chisato had come to the hospital with Maho, to be with her on the day of the operation.

'Thank you for coming,' Tomoko said with feeling.

'Oh, it was fine. I told Maho to go home and I'd let her know when it was over. She only had to be there for the post-operative report, which doctors can only give to a member of the family.'

Maho had come with Saho, who apparently soon became bored and restless. Chisato, being a former flight attendant as well as thoughtful and well-versed in the ways of the world, had been so quick and efficient about sizing up the situation that there was no chance for Maho to even hesitate.

'Maho was truly grateful. She was so impressed at how considerate you were. "That's Aunty Chi-chan for you," she told me. Thank you.'

'Not at all. One in two people get cancer nowadays. It could be me next, so this was a chance to see how things work. I learned a lot.'

This was another of Chisato's good points. Her delicate way of framing things so that the other person never felt in her debt.

'So, is the treatment over then? Did they get all the cancer?'

'Well, it depends.'

Six months earlier, after a routine medical check-up for family at her husband's company clinic, Tomoko had been told that she had a suspected cancer of the uterus. She had gone to several hospitals and private medical clinics for second opinions, among them a doctor who offered a non-surgical treatment using traditional Chinese medicine. After some hesitation, she finally decided to have an operation at a university hospital in Ochanomizu where she had undergone thorough testing. She had been told that it was stage I cancer, but nothing more could be determined without surgery.

'I have to wait for the pathology tests. If the cancer they removed turns out to be stage IA, I won't need anything more. If it's IB, I'll have six months of anti-cancer drug treatment.'

'When will you know?'

'In about two weeks.'

'You won't know anything till then?'

'No. It's rather nerve-racking.'

Tomoko wished she could have had this conversation with her husband. But he seemed to think that having already heard what the doctor had to say, there was no need for further discussion.

'When do you get the results?'

'Thursday, the week after next.'

'Would you like me to go with you?'

'Thank you.' Tomoko was grateful, and happy, for the offer. 'I think I'll be fine on my own, but I might end up asking you.'

'I have time, so feel free to ask.'

When the chips are down, there's nothing like a friend you can count on, thought Tomoko.

'But remember, even if you do need drug treatment, don't brood. Don't forget it's only for six months, and you're lucky they found it at this stage.'

Chisato was also good at offering consolation.

'Yes, you're right.' Despite the leaden feeling in her body, and her frustration at not being able to clean the house, Tomoko felt cheered by this chat.

Chisato had finished eating but made no move to leave. She kept fiddling with her cup and straightening the fork on her plate. Tomoko, who had been telling amusing stories about hospital life – the elderly woman who acted like boss of the ward, and the nurse who was a bit of a character – suddenly realised: Chisato was not her usual self.

'Chisato, do you want to talk about something?'

Chisato looked down, and fiddled with her tea things again, as if she did not know what to say. It was unusual for her.

'Well ... the truth is ... I'm thinking of getting a divorce,' she said.

Tomoko almost stopped breathing in shock.

'Have you been talking about it?'

'Yes, quite a bit. We started around the time you found out about the cancer, so I didn't mention it.'

'But I thought you and Yoshiaki got on well?'

Chisato and her husband were both tall and had always seemed the perfect couple. Yoshiaki worked for the same major airline that Chisato had as a flight attendant, and they had been good friends and colleagues since joining the company at the same time. Yoshiaki had proposed when Chisato turned thirty and was starting to worry about her future. 'I'll do, won't I?' had been his words, which Tomoko had thought charming at the time; manly, and to the point. They had one daughter, Chiaki, who was still at university.

'You were going through all that and still came to see me in hospital so many times – I'm so sorry.' And grateful; for the past few months, while Tomoko had talked about her various treatments and symptomatic therapies, Chisato had simply listened and said nothing, while Tomoko barely listened to her.

'It's all right, really. Listening to you was a distraction. Although it's not the best way to put it.'

When Tomoko had been agonising over whether or not to have an operation, Chisato's words, more than her own family's, had encouraged her the most: 'Personally, I simply want my dear friend to have the latest cancer treatment. I don't want you deciding not to have the operation and regretting it later,' she had said.

'Don't worry about it.'

The reason for Chisato's divorce was all too commonplace.

'Yoshiaki had been seeing someone else for a while, but I had no idea. Then one day I was watching a daytime TV special about mature-age divorces. And I noticed that Yoshiaki ticked all the boxes for a husband who is thinking about divorce.'

According to this programme, the four telltale signs were: (1) Frequently coming home late with little notice. (2) Taking cell phone and smartphone into the bathroom. (3) A keen interest in details of wife's income and savings. (4) Looking at real estate on his computer and smartphone.

'I could understand (1) because of course he would say that he was busy at work or some such thing, when actually he was meeting a woman. Same goes for (2). He wouldn't know when she would contact him and didn't want to be overheard talking with her. (3) starts to happen when the man is thinking about taking concrete steps to a divorce and calculating how much money he'll have to give his wife.'

It was a light-hearted programme, and the studio audience were all laughing. 'I laughed, too,' Chisato said, 'and thought, *Oh, I didn't know that*. But then partway through it stopped being funny and I started crying. Everything up to (3) was true for me. And when I started crying, I realised that deep down I'd had my suspicions for a long time. Only I'd been hiding from it until that moment. Pretending not to know. What an idiot I was.' Chisato gave an embarrassed smile.

Seeing her face, Tomoko took her hand.

'This programme said that if a couple was at stage (4), it was almost impossible to get back together. Up to (2), and there was still a chance.'

In trepidation, Chisato had opened hers and Yoshiaki's shared computer and checked the search history. Sure enough, there was a sizeable string of searches for rental properties and real-estate agencies in the vicinity of the train station near Yoshiaki's office.

'It was a straight line from there.' That night, she had

questioned Yoshiaki, and he immediately began talking about divorce, almost if he had been waiting for the opportunity.

Yoshiaki had transferred to an executive position at a new low-cost airline. 'He changed jobs about a year ago, you see. So I told myself it was only natural he would come home at a different time. But that was where he met this young stewardess – you know, one of those young, bright-eyed, bushy-tailed contract workers.'

Chisato had been a flight attendant herself, and would ordinarily never use derogatory language to speak of others in her profession. Her use of it now was an indication to Tomoko of her friend's state of mind.

'He said things like it was time to think about a different way of life since Chiaki's grown up. He's already moved out. I've got a lawyer and we're in talks.'

'Is this what you want, Chisato?'

'Yes. At first, I thought that if I didn't sign the divorce papers, there could be no divorce. But I was overestimating my power. When I spoke to the lawyer, she told me that's not the case any more.'

'Really? I didn't know that.'

'This lawyer is an expert in divorce issues, and she made it very clear to me. She said that a lot of men see nothing wrong with having a wife and a mistress, and that things could drag on for a very long time while I waited for him to come back to me. But apparently, there are increasingly more cases where divorce is granted if the separation is deemed long enough, even if the other party was the cause – sometimes it only takes a few years.'

'A few years is not long.' Tomoko was aware of how shockingly fast time flew by once children grew up.

Chisato nodded. 'It was a wake-up call. Do I want to be with a man who floats between his mistress and his wife? No, I do not. It's not who I am.'

Tomoko's eyes misted over when Chisato casually asked if she would mind her consulting her about the various things she had to deal with, like divvying up their possessions, money and mortgage on the apartment. Chisato herself, however, seemed if anything more dignified than ever.

All roads lead to Rome, goes the saying, but when Tomoko passed forty-five, she realised that this was an age at which all ailments lead to menopause. That was her experience, anyway. In hindsight, she was still young.

During the early days of summer, she found herself sweating profusely. *Well naturally, because it's summer,* she told herself, but when she got up in the mornings her face, neck and chest would all be soaking wet, and her hair would look as if she'd been caught in a downpour. The discomfort frequently woke her up before dawn, and she would keep a clean T-shirt and towel by her bedside for a quick change. Her pyjamas, when she removed them, felt heavy. Usually, she also went to the bathroom at the same time, which is something she never used to do during the night. Tomoko had always been a bad sleeper, and sometimes did not go back to sleep at all. When her late grandmother used to complain about having to get up twice in the night to wee, it never registered.

To prevent the night sweats, she would sleep with the air

conditioner on, which in turn made her hands and feet cold and puffy. Tomoko hated having to resort to such a wasteful practice as keeping the room cool with the air conditioner while sleeping with a duvet over the lower half of her body. She slept like this not only at the height of summer, but from mid-May through to October.

When Tomoko passed fifty, she and Kazuhiko began sleeping in separate rooms. Not only were their respective body temperatures not in sync, Kazuhiko made noises about Tomoko's getting up and rustling around before dawn. Fortunately, they had a spare room, since both daughters had left home in quick succession to marry and start a new job respectively.

Then came worsening heart palpitations and shortness of breath. Tomoko would wake abruptly in the night, with her heart beating loudly and feeling weird. Positive there must be something wrong with her, she went to doctors, asked around and looked up all kind of things. At first, she suspected a thyroid disorder, but was told by an internist after testing that there was nothing wrong with her thyroid gland. 'There is your age to take into consideration,' the handsome young doctor told her, and for the first time it dawned on her that this might be menopause. So next she saw a gynaecologist, and learned that her female hormones were in spectacular decline. From then on, the symptoms came one after another:

Poor sleep, insomnia = menopause
Dizzy spells, ringing in the ears = menopause
Unexplained itchiness of hands and feet = menopause
Dry skin = menopause

Tomoko was still using a flip phone. She had always resisted her mother-in-law, daughters and even staff at mobile-phone shops, who pushed her to switch to a smartphone. *I can do everything I need with this,* was her riposte. It was, in fact, quite possible to do a lot of research on a flip phone. Whenever she accessed the internet and typed in her ailments, the word 'menopause' always seemed to pop up, along with other possible causes. Eventually the third finger of her right hand began to ache. As if a tendon were being pulled when she bent it. *Surely this can't be menopause too,* she thought, *it must be something to do with overusing the finger.* But when she looked it up on her cell phone, she found at the end of the description of 'tendon sheath inflammation' and 'trigger finger', a sentence that said, 'Also a common symptom that often appears in older women during menopause.'

Even her fingers weren't safe from menopause. Tomoko threw the towel in at this point and accepted that all her problems were related to menopause.

She owned some La Perla lingerie, which she had bought on a trip to Italy during the bubble era with a friend from her student days. The champagne-coloured silk underwear had a delicate lace trim that was sigh-inducing. But it was tucked away in her chest of drawers, and had become discoloured over the years. Although her weight had not changed a great deal, the flimsy garment had almost no corrective power and could not hold Tomoko's flesh in any more; she no longer had the courage to wear it. Nowadays, her cold body was bolstered by the thermal underwear she bought at the Murasaki shop in the Jujo shopping mall.

The first time Tomoko stepped through the door of Murasaki was not long after turning fifty. She had always been aware of the shop as it was often featured in TV specials. According to these programmes, the secret behind its markedly low prices was obtaining irregular-sized or -coloured stock from top-drawer manufacturers. Despite knowing this, it had never occurred to Tomoko to go there. She had seen the large cardboard boxes that always lined the pavement outside the shopfront, sporting handwritten signs such as 'socks for ¥60' and 'pantyhose for ¥99'. And she had seen, too, the crowds of senior citizens from the neighbourhood who rummaged through the boxes with their faces almost buried in them. *I could never do that,* she used to think, *the day I do, it will be over for me as a woman.*

In any case, Tomoko didn't wear socks and bought her stockings in bulk at a department store in Shinjuku whenever she was there. She believed that it was far more economical to buy good-quality items and take care of them.

One March a few years earlier, however, she had had to attend the funeral of Kazuhiko's boss. The season was still cold and she anticipated having to stand around in a draughty place, so she went to the department stores to find thick black tights to go with her mourning clothes. But with spring so close there were none in stock anywhere. Upon her return to Jujo, she was walking through the shopping mall when Murasaki caught her eye and she stopped in her tracks. 'Er, would you happen to have any very warm tights?' she timidly approached a female assistant to ask. 'I'm going to a funeral.'

'Oh, yes, we have some good ones in stock,' the woman, a

little older than Tomoko herself, replied cheerfully. 'They're warm and cosy!'

The black tights she produced were extremely thick and fleece-lined, the like of which Tomoko had never seen in any department store. They were very cheap to boot at ¥299. Hence Tomoko entered the shop that she had been avoiding for so long, and added thick socks for wearing at home and a fleecy, long-sleeve granny undershirt to her purchases.

The extra-thick black tights did a sterling job of protecting Tomoko's legs from the bitter cold north wind during the funeral, keeping her warm as toast the whole time. Tomoko had been a big fan of Murasaki ever since. She always stopped to browse whenever she was shopping in the mall, and particularly liked their range of warm winter underwear. No doubt it was because she fit the target clientele, of middle-aged and older women. Before she knew it, Tomoko had accumulated a drawer full of unopened underwear from Murasaki, to the extent that her daughters teased her.

Passing through the doorway of this shop always filled her with a sense of peace. As if being there bestowed on her the freedom to admit to her age: she was an 'old lady' and enjoyed the warmth and comfort of her old-lady underwear. Wearing it put a spring in her step. Men had showered attention on her in the days of the bubble era, and she had been bound by the notion of having to be eternally feminine ever since, or at least a beautiful mother. The chance to permit herself to be an old lady came as a great relief. And then she got cancer.

*

After Chisato's revelation about the divorce, Tomoko began receiving late-night phone calls from her. She and Kazuhiko no longer shared a bedroom, so she felt no inhibition about taking long phone calls. It was like being a student again. Unlike their student days, however, most of Tomoko's and Chisato's conversation now centred around the thorny topic of money.

'We married at thirty, right? So we're splitting everything we saved over the next twenty-five years, fifty-fifty, down the middle. I was mostly a full-time housewife, but he could only earn what he did thanks to me.'

'Really. But do you know how much he saved before you married? I'd have difficulty coming up with that myself.'

'That's what you'd expect, isn't it? But he remembers a surprising amount, actually. Like the fact he had about three million in savings, and claims that apart from the monetary gifts we received, he and his parents paid for the entire wedding. He brings up things I've completely forgotten about.'

Chisato was stylish, and had always dressed in good-quality clothing and accessories that clearly cost money. But she had never spoken with Tomoko before about the details of her financial status.

'I wouldn't have expected that. If anything, I thought Yoshiaki'd be quite indifferent to such things.' Tomoko recalled Yoshiaki never letting them pay when they were single and the three of them had gone out to eat together. It was partly the times, but also because Yoshiaki was the type of man who didn't let women pay.

'Me neither. But divorce can really change people.'

Tomoko noted with concern the self-mocking note in Chisato's voice.

'I went to a lecture on divorce and money the other day. It was given by that woman you sometimes see on TV, you know, Suko Kurofune?'

'What? Never heard of her.'

'You can find anything on the internet nowadays. Anyway, my takeaway from this lecture was some rough calculations for how much I can receive, along with future living costs. This was based on the typical amount for a middle-aged couple. From a financial perspective, naturally you're better off not getting divorced.'

'Well, yes, naturally.'

'If we stayed married, we'd receive a pension of two hundred and thirty thousand yen a month in total; one hundred and thirty thousand yen from the National Pension Plan and one hundred thousand yen from the Employees' Pension Fund. Average monthly expenses for a mature-aged unemployed couple are less than two hundred and fifty thousand yen, so it shouldn't be too difficult to survive by supplementing this from savings.'

'That's reassuring.' Though this was about her friend, Tomoko felt relieved that her own family was presently not threatened with divorce.

'Of course that doesn't cover expenses in case of illness, nursing care or travel,' Chisato continued. 'We both married at thirty. He joined the company straight out of university, worked for thirty-three years, and was married to me for twenty-five of those. So we can break that down into a ratio of thirty-three to twenty-five, roughly four to three. Our pension, savings and retirement benefit will all be split four-three. The pension won't give me much. We get half each from the National Pension Plan fund, which is sixty-five thousand yen each, but the Employees' Pension Plan will be divided four-three. That gives Yoshiaki fifty-seven thousand yen and me forty-three thousand. But we can't get this money until we're sixty-five. And then we have to figure in the fact that for the next five years, until Yoshiaki turns sixty, he'll be supporting this new woman so that proportion will be deducted too.'

'For only five years?'

'Yes. Then there's our savings. Yoshiaki's retirement benefit from his previous job, combined with all our other savings, also gets divided up four-three. Yoshiaki receives 11.42 million and me 8.57 million.'

Chisato's daughter had gone to a private high school and the couple had bought a condominium in pricey Shinjuku Ward. *Trust an airline company to pay the kind of money where you could still have twenty million saved up after paying for all of that,* thought Tomoko.

'But apparently, in single-person households, women spend more than men. This month my average spend was about a hundred and fifty thousand yen. Which means that if, like me, a woman gets divorced and has no pension for the first ten years, even if she works part-time and earns seventy thousand a month, she will have to break into her savings to supplement this, and after eight years will have hardly anything left! I'll run through almost all my savings before I even receive my pension!'

'In just eight years! But you'll only be sixty-three then!' Tomoko's hand flew to her mouth in astonishment.

It was painful to picture Chisato with no money – the least likely person Tomoko could imagine that happening to.

'There's also the question of what to do with the flat. Since we have a child it's likely that I can stay there and finish paying off the mortgage. Yoshiaki is saying he wants to count what he's paid so far, as compensation to me for pain and suffering. At first I thought that would be better than having no home, but I don't know how long I can afford to keep paying the mortgage.'

Tomoko was stunned.

'Sometimes I wonder, why did this happen? It feels like everything changed all at once.'

As it would. It was all Tomoko could do to offer any comfort. 'Talk to me about anything you want; if there's nothing else I can do, at least I can listen.'

Chisato finished up the call with the advice that Tomoko should thoroughly review her own financial situation. Which was why, the next day, Tomoko opened their savings account bank book to check the balance. And was appalled to discover that the account, which she had thought was in quite good shape, was almost depleted.

She could see how it happens; all of a sudden, one day the money runs out. But it wasn't as if she had failed in business, or was a gambler. She hadn't been extravagant or the victim of a scam. She had simply been leading a modest life. That was all.

Her mother-in-law had given her a copy of Motoko Hani's

A Model Family Budget Book when they were first married, and gave her this advice: 'You don't have to scrimp, but it's good to at least record all your spending.'

Tomoko came from the Chugoku region in Western Japan. Her father had been a local government bureaucrat and the family lived in a large house inherited from her grandparents. Although they were not particularly wealthy, paying rent was not an issue and they often received produce from the neighbours, so the concept of economising had not been foremost in their minds. Still, country life was not as cheap as people think. Families need not just one but two or even three cars to get about, plus there are all kinds of social obligations that don't exist in the city, which can add up to more than you might imagine. The monetary gifts, for example, whenever a memorial service is held for a relative or neighbour, and donations to shrines and neighbourhood associations when festivals are held, or the matching summer cotton *yukata* that must be made on such occasions. Gifts of money were also obligatory whenever a relative went to university or married. Naturally, Tomoko had been the recipient of such gifts, too.

Everybody seemed to know everyone else's financial situation, and there would be backbiting about anyone who failed to join in, or was stingy with food, drink or vehicles. Economising was never held up as a virtue.

When Kotoko, Kazuhiko and her father-in-law had visited Tomoko's home to pay their respects to her parents, they had brought a box of confectionery – sweet potato *kintsuba* – as a gift. It was true that the families had already agreed on holding a simple, modest wedding, but Tomoko's parents were nonetheless taken aback by the modesty of this gift. Such that Tomoko passed into family lore amongst all her relatives as the bride who went for the price of a box of kintsuba.

She was initially bewildered by city ways, but then began to see Tokyoites' characteristic indifference to other people as liberating. Akin to being free to loll about at home and stretch out exactly as she pleased. If she had done anything of the sort in her hometown a neighbour would be quite capable of entering through the unlocked front door and saying, 'What are you lying about in the middle of the day for?'

On the other hand, her mother-in-law had taught her how to keep a household budget, and she had become more conscious of saving money. That did not prevent her from being dumbfounded, however, when Kazuhiko consulted his mother about buying a car after the birth of their first child, and they decided on a cheap, light car. Her parents would never have stinted themselves on buying such a vehicle for a second or even third car.

Tomoko missed being able to grumble on the phone to her late mother about the stinginess of people in Tokyo. Still, it was thanks to these habits that they had accumulated ¥8 million in savings. Which was now fast disappearing. They still had ¥8 million when their eldest daughter, Maho, graduated from high school, but ¥5 million had subsequently gone towards the girls' education, and then came Maho's wedding. The young couple had said they would finance it themselves – and it was by no means an extravagant affair – but the various sundry expenses mounted up to around ¥1 million: there was a dinner for both families, and extra money for Maho's wedding dress when she found she wanted something better that did not fit her budget, and obligatory cash reimbursements for relatives who came from the country to attend the wedding.

Then Tomoko's mother and Kazuhiko's father had died in quick succession and they had had to pay their share of hospital and funeral expenses, which were split amongst their siblings. There was also Tomoko's hospital expenses. The operation was covered by health insurance, but all the tests she had had done at several other hospitals first had cost more than anticipated.

The fact was, Kazuhiko's salary had also hardly increased in the last ten years. The medium-size precision-machinery manufacturer he worked for had been in the doldrums ever since the recession caused by the global financial crisis, and had been the target of numerous approaches for a merger. Added to which Kazuhiko had not been promoted, as might have been expected, to section manager after turning fifty. Even now, he remained in the position of deputy chief, an ambiguous title that gave Tomoko no clue of its importance in the hierarchy.

On top of everything else, Tomoko worried about how much they would have to spend on nursing care for her mother-in-law, Kotoko, in future. The mere thought gave her a headache. Kazuhiko had a younger brother who lived in Osaka and had taken over his wife's family business. He wasn't an officially adopted son as such, but was treated pretty much like one – obviously he would have responsibilities there. Tomoko only ever saw him at weddings and funerals. She didn't know what the brothers had decided between them concerning their mother, or whether they had even had any kind of discussion at all. But she hesitated to bring up the topic in case anyone said, 'Okay, you take care of it please, Tomoko,' and hence was pretending to ignore the issue.

Money had been spilling out from between their fingers, and without realising it, there was now only just under ¥1 million remaining.

Oh, to have twenty million in savings like Chisato! It was a luxury Tomoko could only dream of.

A week after her discharge from hospital, Tomoko was finally able to go out shopping. She had been told not to ride a bicycle for a month, and so she walked at a slow pace to the Jujo shopping mall, where her first stop was Murasaki.

'Hello there, you're out of hospital.' The female shop assistant greeted her with a smile. It seems she remembered Tomoko's last visit to buy several pairs of button-up pyjamas before her operation.

When Tomoko mentioned that she was unable to ride a bicycle for a while, the assistant promptly recommended a shopping cart with wheels, commonly known as a granny trolley. Murasaki had a supply of these and other such items in a corner of the store. The cart cost ¥890, and the assistant also remembered to give Tomoko a ¥200 discount as a congratulatory gift for her discharge from hospital.

With so many elderly customers, no wonder she's quick to understand what I need, thought Tomoko. She was feeling one step closer to old age. Her illness, in combination with the news of her best friend's divorce and the shocking review of the Mikuriya family finances, had brought about a major upheaval in her mental landscape.

To begin with, she was facing the reality of having to start saving again for old age. Then there was the realisation that as things stood, divorce from her husband was not possible for her. She had never given this any thought before, but being confronted with his complete inability to do anything around the house upon her return from hospital had been a trigger for her to reflect on her life: *He's gruff, but not uncaring, and he's worked diligently to provide for the girls and me. His mother is a strong woman, and the girls are attached to her. But what will life be like once he retires? How can I go on as I do now, cooking him three meals a day, cleaning and doing the laundry every single day, and having to see his face all the time?*

She sighed. The outlook was not good, if what Chisato had said about income projections for single women after a mature-age divorce were true. *The hard truth is, I have to put with him, no matter what.* Tomoko had never thought about divorcing before, but the realisation that she had no choice unsettled her. Her resentment grew at times such as dinner, when they ate together in silence. *Why does he never show any sign of appreciation, when he can't even cook?* And on the weekends, when all he ever seemed to do was sleep and go out occasionally to play golf – his only hobby – with friends, Tomoko would have to wait for him to come home and then cook, just as she did on weekdays. *Will life still go on like this once he retires? For ever?*

Tomoko's eye was caught by a display of discount vegetables outside the supermarket midway down the shopping mall. She picked them up to look; a whole cabbage was going for ¥100, half a Chinese cabbage for ¥100 and a bag of onions for ¥100. She put a selection in her basket, then headed for the meat section. Today, chicken breast was selling for ¥48 per 100g, ¥10 cheaper than usual. She chose a jumbo-size pack with four pieces, and also picked up two packets of scrap pork selling for ¥98 per 100g.

The Jujo shopping mall often featured on TV as it was well known for the many speciality shops selling ready-made side dishes for meals. There were shops that sold chicken balls for ¥10 each, and chicken cutlets larger than the palm of your hand for ¥160. Everything was delicious, and Tomoko often shopped here before her operation. Making deep-fried food for two was a lot of work, and she had thought that they were at the stage of life where taking some shortcuts could be justified. She would get one shop-bought dish and serve it with homemade rice, miso soup and a small bowl of something else.

That was before. Ready-made food was a luxury they couldn't afford any more. At home she immediately began processing the chicken breasts. First, she removed the skin from all four pieces, then chopped up two of these to put in the food processor and turn into mincemeat, which she divided into 100g portions to freeze. The rest of the meat she sliced and put in a marinade of sake and ginger, which she had heard on TV made the meat tender. This, too, she divided into small portions to freeze. Then she separated the pork similarly and froze some. Next, she chopped half the cabbage to make a coleslaw salad, which she stored in a Tupperware container in the fridge.

At this point, weariness overtook her. Tomoko sat down and propped her cheeks on her hands as she leaned on the dining table. This all used to be a breeze when she was younger. She would shop for the evening meal on the way home from her part-time job, cook dinner, feed, bathe and put her daughters to bed, then wait for her husband who was late getting home. She had always assumed that once the girls left home, she would have time to herself at last. But here she was having to mince chicken again – at her age!

Tomoko surveyed the remaining half-cabbage, Chinese cabbage and onions in the kitchen that were still not packed away. The dirty food processor was in the sink, and cutting boards and knives were lying about waiting to be washed. A sigh rose up from deep within. *How much longer will I have to keep doing this for?*

'Can't be helped. We're poor. There's no money,' she mumbled to herself. Tears rose in her eyes.

Dinner the night before had also been chicken breast. Tomoko had served chicken and egg on rice – made from sliced chicken breast and onion – miso soup and salad.

'This meat's a bit tough,' Kazuhiko had commented. He was not a picky eater and usually ate what he was served without a word. It was probably only a throwaway comment, said without thinking or any ill will, but Tomoko was furious. She almost threw her chopsticks at him. In fact, she did so in her head. In reality, however, she said nothing and simply left the table.

It was true, the meat was tough. *Maybe I overcooked it, or chopped it the wrong way,* she mused. In any case – it wasn't good.

It wasn't a problem with the meat itself. One of Tomoko's English teachers had once told her that she was surprised to discover that chicken-thigh meat was more expensive than breast meat in Japan, because in her home country of Australia, breast meat was the more expensive. Breast meat was much tastier and healthier than thigh meat, depending on how you cooked it, of course. In short, it's how you prepare and cook the meat that matters. It was a sorry thing, Tomoko thought, for a veteran housewife of her experience to produce tough chicken meat. *And I'm supposedly experienced enough to teach others how to cook osechi.*

She knew that her preparation had not been perfect, but in one week she would learn the results of her pathology test, and simply could not focus. If she needed to have radiation therapy, she would have to go into hospital, and feel unwell even after being discharged. What would Kazuhiko do then? For six months? Their health insurance would cover medical expenses, but if she was unable to do the cooking or housework for a prolonged period, they would run through their savings in no time.

Tomoko felt another niggle in her lower abdomen, where she'd had surgery. The net effect of her cheerless train of thought had been to make her feel as if it was all inevitable. She was better off not trying to talk herself out of this mood, so when the news actually came, she wouldn't be as devastated.

*

'These places are always so busy. Is there a shortage of doctors, or clinics?' Chisato murmured, casting a look at the TV in the waiting room. She and Tomoko were waiting to hear Tomoko's pathology results from her operation. Though the appointment was for 2 p.m., twenty minutes had passed with no sign of her being called. Women ranging in age from their twenties to eighties sat awkwardly on the bench sofas that crammed the waiting room.

'Sorry,' said Tomoko.

'I didn't mean it like that. I was the one who insisted on coming. We can chat while we wait,' said Chisato.

When Tomoko had emailed Chisato and told her that she was nervous about going to hear the test results alone, Chisato had immediately offered to go with her. Of course she hadn't forced herself on Tomoko.

'This might be our daily routine when we're older,' Tomoko answered with a weak smile. 'How's it going with Yoshiaki? Are things moving along?'

'I thought everything would go quicker after the decision to split all the money down the middle. But now we're stuck on the issue of child support and Chiaki's education. He originally said he would take care of both. Now he's saying that he shouldn't have to pay child support because she's already twenty.'

'What? But Chiaki's still at university!'

'That's right. But now he's saying because he'll pay half her education fees, he can't pay child support.'

'That's too unfair.'

'People can become heartless in the face of a break-up. I

expect his new woman put all sorts of ideas into his head. All of a sudden he's become grudging.'

Money is probably something that will always be in dispute until the very end, thought Tomoko.

'What bothers me most is, I think Yoshiaki might be getting used to this situation.'

'What do you mean?'

'I said before, didn't I, how the lawyer told me that men quite enjoy flitting between their wives and mistresses? Well, I have the feeling that Yoshiaki is finding it not so bad to go back and forward between his new young woman and old wife with a sweet daughter.'

'That's ludicrous.' Tomoko felt disgusted at the idea of Yoshiaki behaving so contemptuously to his wife, and women in general.

'It's how he comes across, whining about how hard he has it, while he bounces back and forth between two households – after so many years together I can read him. But I can't put up with that. I've made the decision to separate. I'm not going back on it.'

'That's right.' Tomoko nodded in agreement. But she had a feeling that maybe Chisato was not as exasperated as she was making out. Perhaps she, too, was having difficulty letting go. Perhaps she was the one becoming used to this situation? Behind the complaints, maybe a part of her felt reassured. Tomoko stole a glance at her friend. *I can't blame her,* she thought. *They were a couple for twenty-five years.*

'Mrs Mikuriya, Mrs Mikuriya. Please come to examination room three,' called a young nurse in a high-pitched voice.

Chisato's face went tense. 'Tomoko, that's you – you're up.'

Tomoko squeezed Chisato's hand. They went into the examination room together like a pair of schoolgirls holding hands tightly. Tomoko could sense that Chisato, too, was frightened. She found that amusing, since Chisato had grandly insisted on coming with her in case she collapsed, but now the moment was here, Chisato was the one who was quailing. Tomoko didn't mind, she knew that her friend's fear was the flip side of her concern for her.

Much to Tomoko's surprise, the moment she entered the room, she instantly felt lighter. Maybe it was the atmosphere, to which her sensitivity had been honed by repeated visits here. It felt different today. Cheerful, somehow. The young doctor and nurse by his side no longer had a subdued, worried aura about them. The tension was gone.

'Please take a seat, Mrs Mikuriya.'

'I brought a friend with me today.'

'Please have a seat, too.'

Tomoko and Chisato sat down side by side.

'We have your pathology results from the other day.'

The doctor was getting straight to the point. Smiling, he opened Tomoko's chart.

This is it, thought Tomoko. She had almost never seen him smile before.

'Congratulations! You were stage IA!'

'What?' Tomoko squeaked in surprise, despite having anticipated this outcome from his expression.

'The cancer we removed was about one centimetre in diameter. It was stage IA.'

'Tomoko, thank goodness,' said Chisato, her voice thick with emotion.

Tomoko could not speak. She turned to her friend and nodded. Immediately turning back to the doctor she asked, 'What about radiation therapy?'

'No need,' he said, then proceeded to outline the schedule for her future treatment; a monthly check-up for a few months, then a CT scan once a year.

Tomoko's mind, however, was already far away. In her head a voice – perhaps her own, perhaps someone else's, she couldn't tell – was saying *This is the beginning. This is where it all starts.*

'I see, so that's why there are two of you here today,' said Suko Kurofune to a nervous-looking Tomoko and Chisato seated in front of her.

After learning the results of the pathology test, the two had stopped for tea at a café near Ochanomizu Station. In the course of their conversation and listening to Chisato speak of her experience, Tomoko had begun to think that it might be a good idea for her, too, to consult a financial planner about her own situation.

'Excuse me, after hearing about you from Ms Kono, I became very keen to hear your opinion. When I enquired, I learned that you also do group consultations.'

'That's right. Many people are nervous about private consultations with a financial planner because they think that they have to report every last penny of their savings, but an initial visit with a friend can help lower the barrier to coming along. Quite a few financial planners only offer individual consultations, but personally, I believe that a consultation of any kind is a good start. Once the conversation gets deeper, some people find they prefer a one-on-one situation.'

Tomoko had difficulty picturing Ms Kurofune, with her lively eyes and cheerful, amiable manner, as the same woman who often appeared on TV yelling 'Eight times twelve is the magic number!' She began to relax a little. Her situation was different to Chisato's, whose divorce was almost finalised. The feelings that were eating away at her were not something she could express in words as such. However, their lack of savings did seem worth asking about. And there were other nebulous fears and gripes lurking in the back of her mind, which would never go away if she continued to dwell on them alone. Finding out that the cancer was stage IA had lifted her mood, which in turn spurred her on to be more proactive about dealing with her other worries.

Ms Kurofune's consultation fee was ¥6,000 an hour, which split between the two of them came to ¥3,000 each. It was a substantial amount, but Tomoko wasn't expecting a miracle solution to her problems. She wanted to prove to herself that she was making an effort. That alone would not be a bad return on her ¥3,000.

'Let's begin with hearing from you, Tomoko Mikuriya, about your situation, shall we?'

'All right, but I'm not sure I can explain it properly. Please excuse me if I don't convey it well.'

Tomoko told her story. How after hearing about Chisato's situation she had checked her own family finances and discovered that their savings had dwindled to less than ¥1 million, how her cancer treatment was over for the most part but she had lost confidence in her physical strength, and was not sure if she had the stamina to economise as she had when she was younger, how her daughters had families and jobs and she did not want to burden them in the future, and how she had no idea about the cost of caring for her mother-in-law in future.

'There's actually something else, too, which I haven't even told Chisato yet.' Tomoko looked at Chisato to acknowledge her before continuing. 'Miho, my younger daughter, came to see us a few days ago, and mentioned in passing that she is seeing someone now.'

'That's lovely, isn't it? You must be happy that she wanted to tell her mother about it,' Chisato interjected brightly.

'Yes, but it's not like Miho to tell us this kind of thing. She's never said anything like it to me before. For her to make the effort to come all the way home and tell us means that she is thinking seriously about marriage.'

'You're worried that there might be the cost of a wedding as well, are you not?'

Trust the money expert and financial planner to immediately pinpoint the issue.

'Yes, I am. When my elder daughter married, she and her husband said they'd pay for it themselves, but there were still expenses that cropped up for us and it ended up costing rather a lot. My daughters are precious, and I want to give Miho the chance to have a wedding without feeling constrained. But so much depends on her boyfriend. For all we know he might be from a wealthy family that wants a lavish wedding. How much could we subsidise in that case? I couldn't sleep last night for thinking about it.'

'I do understand,' Ms Kurofune said, lifting her head from the memo that she had been taking detailed notes on while listening to Tomoko.

'Let's start with the issue of your second daughter's marriage.'

She's getting straight to it, thought Tomoko. *Just as well, since there are two of us to get through in just one hour. It'll be a big help to get as much advice as possible.*

'... and put that aside for the moment. This is not your problem, Tomoko, rather it's your daughter's. Maybe the young man's parents do want a luxurious wedding. If that's the case it's for the young couple to deal with, not for you to worry over. Your daughter is an adult and you need to be clear about making that distinction. Not to mention there is no point in worrying over it now when you haven't even met him. Besides, I feel that once your basic problem is solved, this matter will naturally resolve itself.'

'Um ... okay,' said Tomoko uncertainly.

Though not completely happy with her ability to be this succinct in making that distinction, Tomoko was nevertheless relieved to be told that it wasn't her problem.

'The same applies for your mother-in-law. Caregiving should not impact in such a way as to create a cycle of poverty, I believe. Children have an obligation to care for their parents, but the interpretation of this under the law is that it should be within the scope of their financial means. If caregiving is a source of financial strain, a parent can be classified in a separate household and thus become eligible for welfare assistance. In the case of this too, Tomoko, if we can resolve the main issue in your life, then your other options should become clear.'

At this point, Ms Kurofune paused to take a mouthful of tea from the cup on her desk. Almost as if to indicate that they were about to get down to brass tacks.

'After listening to you, there's something that bothers me. You came to consult me about your family finances because you want to economise, but don't have confidence in your physical condition, am I correct? But as you spoke you mentioned your husband several times, saying that he cannot do any housework, you have to do everything and he is indifferent to home matters.'

Tomoko had to admit she was right. She had tried to avoid complaining about Kazuhiko since today was supposed to be a consultation about family finances. And it wasn't as if he were a spendthrift, or had a negative impact on their savings. But somehow, she had let it slip.

'Isn't it true that you are dissatisfied with your husband?'

'Well, yes, there is that. We've been together for so many years, and I think it's fair to say we are both increasingly dissatisfied with each other. But it's the same for all mature couples, isn't it? And besides ...' Tomoko glanced at Chisato sitting beside her. She had not said much about her husband, partly out of concern for her best friend, whose divorce was imminent. Chisato seemed to intuit this, and gave a slight nod, as if to say *It's okay.*

Tomoko had met Kazuhiko through a friend. A serious young man who never said an unnecessary word, she saw in him a man like her father, with all the modesty and restraint characteristic of someone born a generation earlier in the mid-Showa period. Tomoko was fed up with frivolous, flashy young men from the era in which she came of age. Perhaps she had too many illusions. The man she had dreamed would be taciturn but dependable in times of need was simply silent.

'When I heard about Chisato's situation, it made me think that a divorce was out of the question for me. We could split the retirement allowance and pension between us, but as a woman I would still be at a disadvantage. Not to mention that we don't have any decent savings.'

'It's true that I did create a financial life plan for Chisato Kono to follow. But it was taking a long view on the reality of her situation, and with the hope that she would follow it steadily. It was never for the purpose of leading a backward-looking life.'

'But to divorce like that?'

'I am not recommending divorce to you, Ms Mikuriya. I simply do not want you to have the idea that you must put up with anything for financial reasons. Please put the money issues aside, and take the time to think carefully about what you really want.'

'All right.'

'Divorce is not the end of life, but the start of a new one.'

Tomoko turned to Chisato. 'That's true. I'm sorry, Chisato.'

'What are you talking about? If anyone, I understand how you feel.'

They smiled at each other.

'Let's get down to the specifics then, shall we?' said Ms Kurofune. 'I think it would be good to start with what you can both do now.'

Tomoko returned from shopping and put away her purchases in the refrigerator. Next, she opened her purse, removed the receipts and counted the notes. After turning these to all face the same way, she put them back in her purse and turned her attention to the receipts. She stared long at them, checking how much she had spent, before attaching them to the fridge door with a magnet. This was one of Suko Kurofune's tips – a way of never forgetting to use up everything in the fridge.

'Simply checking your purse and taking out receipts to organise them can be very effective. Instead of bending over backwards to cook money-saving dishes and buying heavily discounted ingredients, focus on using up everything you purchase, and don't overbuy. But buy ready-prepared food when you are tired. Your health is the most important thing right now.'

'Are you sure? I can really do that?'

'Yes, you can. You brought up two fine daughters, didn't you? Your food expenses should be less than what they used to be, and no matter what you buy, it's better than eating out. Concentrate instead on economising a little at the end of the month. Don't go shopping in the last week, think of recipes to use up all the leftovers and stock of ingredients you have. The average home usually has enough food in the kitchen to last a week or so. It's a simple way of making a difference.'

'I see,' Tomoko had replied, remembering the day she had come home from hospital and managed to prepare dinner easily enough despite thinking that there was nothing in the house to eat.

'Start with what is easy to do. And one more thing. How about setting a few days a week when you and your husband eat dinner separately?'

'What?'

'You said before that you go to an English class, don't you? You could ask your husband to get his own dinner on that night. He could cook for himself, or eat out. You may be a couple, but it might be good to give each other some space occasionally, and see how you want to spend your old age.'

How much easier that would be! Tomoko had thought. Her classmates usually went out for dinner somewhere after the lesson, but she never joined them because she had to get home and cook her husband's dinner.

'You must put an end to this situation of seeing yourself as sacrificing yourself for him. It will only drive both of you to unhappiness.'

As she prepared the dinner, Tomoko recalled Chisato's deep nod of agreement when Ms Kurofune had said this. Today's meal was miso soup, rice, tofu topped with *natto*, and sauteed liver with Chinese chive for the main dish. The miso soup was left over from this morning, while the tofu and natto simply required removing from the packet. Then all she had to do was cook the main dish. Putting together a meal composed of soup, rice and two side dishes, one of which came from a packet, was another of Ms Kurofune's tips.

In addition to the tofu and natto, on her shopping trip that day Tomoko had bought other items which could be served up simply by opening the package; vinegared *mozuku* seaweed, *mekabu* seaweed, egg tofu and bamboo leaf-shaped *kamaboko*. Now all she had to do was come up with a main dish. But she knew that when necessary, she could buy something tasty from the mall.

Kazuhiko arrived home after eight. As usual, he changed out of his work clothes and then sat down at the dining table, reaching for the TV remote control at the same time.

'Can you wait before turning on the TV? I want to talk about something first.'

'What?' Obediently he released the remote control and looked at Tomoko with those big round eyes, so unusual in a man. Nothing clouded his expression. He had not the slightest inkling of Tomoko's discontent or opinion about him. In retrospect, Tomoko realised that it had been a very long time since she and her husband had looked at each other like this to talk.

'You know that I go to an English class on Thursdays, don't you?'

'Yeah.' Kazuhiko didn't really remember, but nodded anyway.

'Well from now on, I'd like you to get your own dinner on Thursdays,' Tomoko said all at once, without taking breath.

'What do you mean, get it myself?'

'I mean that literally. You can cook for yourself or go out to eat. Or eat at your mother's if you want. I want to be free of having to make dinner on Thursdays.'

'Why?' Kazuhiko asked with a sullen expression.

'The other students all go out to dinner with the teacher afterwards and they talk about all sorts of things. I've always wanted to go, too, but never could because I have to cook your dinner. But I've decided I'm not going to hold back any more.'

Kazuhiko looked like a child being forced to wait for the food before him on the table.

'Being ill has made me think. I don't want to live a life where I have to put up with everything all the time. I think it's reasonable that you let me take one day off a week, don't you? That's why.'

'All right,' Kazuhiko cut in brusquely, reaching for the TV remote control once again.

Tomoko let out her breath. She had actually wanted to take off two days a week. And tell him that the English class was not the only reason, but because the housework and cooking were also becoming more and more of a burden every year.

'Take it one step at a time. Don't rush,' Suko Kurofune had said in conclusion. 'Don't think you can change everything at once.' This came to Tomoko's mind now. *Yes, one step at a time. If Kazuhiko has to eat alone even just once a week, he might begin to notice or think of things by himself.* It was a far better tactic than outright opposition.

Tomoko picked up her chopsticks and began to eat mouthfuls of the same food her husband had already begun chewing. The sauteed liver and chives were salty, and stuck in her throat, but she chewed on it vigorously and swallowed it down.

6

A Family That Economises

Not long ago I had to make a decision about something that comes around every two years. You guessed it – the smartphone contract! Mine was nearly up and I wasn't sure what to do next. As you all know, this has a big impact on daily expenses for the next two years, so it's a major decision.

My boyfriend (art college internship design company) is one of those people who enjoys changing over their smartphone. He always chooses the most expensive, feature-rich version of the latest iPhone every time there's a new release. And he stays with Company S as his provider, because of their aggressive promotion campaigns to replace old models every time a new one comes out. It worries me what that means financially, when I think we might be married one day.

But this is what he says: 'People are always looking at their smartphone or fiddling with them. The way I see it, a smartphone is the thing I spend the most time on in my daily life. Most of my books and music are electronic or downloaded. So even though mine might be a little more expensive, I don't think it's such an extravagance if you calculate the cost per day over a year. It's not like buying jewellery that you only use a few times a year.'

I guess that's one way to think about it. But I also wonder if maybe he's trying to tell me we don't need an engagement ring?

Anyway, back to the topic. My boyfriend studied in Australia for about six months when he was a student, and I think travelling in Asia at that time shaped his ideas. He told me: 'People always started talking to me at Starbucks in Singapore, to ask if they could borrow my Wi-Fi, or where I was from. Then they'd ask me to watch their things while they went to the restroom. These were people I'd only just met. In a foreign country, and they weren't even Japanese. Singapore's a safe place, and Japanese people are generally trusted there, but after a while I realised why they trusted me. It was my Apple laptop and latest-model iPhone. In the past people used to judge others based on their shoes or clothes, or if they carried a brand-name bag. Not now. These days even rich people wear tatty sneakers, T-shirts and denim. Clothes don't matter any more, gadgets are what counts. Gadgets are universal, a passport to a shared language and sensibility.'

I don't think that's the whole story, but he does have a point.

For the last two years I've used an iPhone 5s that I bought from Company D when I replaced my previous smartphone. At the time it didn't seem outdated. I like the design and have almost no complaints, so I thought about keeping it. But with rumours of an iPhone 8 release soon, I wondered if maybe it's time to get an iPhone 7, or at least an iPhone 6s.

The thing that decided me was Company D's policy. When I asked about upgrades and plans, I was told that tariffs would be much the same whether I upgraded or not. (This might be coincidence, but I also didn't have a very good impression of the woman I spoke to on the phone.) It seems to be standard now, that there are no benefits to being a loyal, long-term customer with telecommunications service providers any more. Major companies and newer start-ups all push plans that allow you to transfer from other providers and keep the same number. There are a lot more of these available now, too. It's not just the big companies in the market, any more. You can do things that used to be impossible, like buy cheap smartphones, SIM-free smartphones and a choice of SIM cards.

So the question is, what is the cheapest way to buy and run your smartphone? And which company is best?

Having written thus far all in one go, Miho Mikuriya let out a long breath. She read back over what she had written carefully, from the beginning. *Hmm, not bad,* she thought, *but too long. It's supposed to be about finding the best-value provider, but I took my time getting to the main subject. And the words are so tightly packed the text looks almost pitch-black. What Shohei said is interesting, though. He just came out with that when I told him I was going to write a post about smartphones tonight.*

After Miho broke up with Daiki, who she had been going out with since university, she started seeing Shohei Numata, the guy she had met at the Suko Kurofune seminar. His slim, clean-cut but not too good-looking appearance appealed to her, and they had grown close after Miho asked his advice about looking for a flat in Jujo, where her parents lived. Going out to look at places for Miho to rent became their excuse for a date. And now that Miho lived in Jujo, with Shohei in Akabane, they were only a five-minute bicycle ride away from each other.

Shohei, however, was not especially interested in economising. He had vague ideas about starting his own business in future, and simply liked going to workshops. He was always on the lookout for inexpensive courses, seminars or breakfast meetings to attend, and would sign up for anything if he had the time.

Nevertheless, he was understanding of Miho's desire to economise. During the week they mostly saw each other at either of their places, because that was cheaper than going out to eat. In fact, when Miho was moving, he had even said, 'Why don't you come and live with me?' She wasn't sure if he were serious or joking, but in any case, was hesitant to move in with somebody before marriage, especially living so close to her parents.

Despite not going out much, Miho found Shohei to be good company and fun to talk with. He often came up with topics for her blog as well, which readers seemed to pick up on, for she would sometimes find comments such as 'Your boyfriend is a funny guy' or 'I agree with your boyfriend.'

Miho always aimed for a direct, conversational tone in her blog, but she wasn't too sure about this post. *Readers will be bored before I even get to the point,* she worried. Placing her hand on the mouse, she resolutely cut a block of text, starting from *My boyfriend* up to *so I thought about keeping it.*

It's a pity to cut so much, she thought, *but not everything is lost.* She decided to save the cut section for another time. Turning back to the screen, she continued.

In this post I'll limit myself to discussing the most economical way to buy and operate an iPhone. Don't get me wrong, I'm not religious about Apple and I don't consider the iPhone to be the ultimate in smartphones. I could tell you about my sister, for example, who has a slightly older Android model (Nexus 5) from Google for less than ¥2,000 a month, which she gets from Company Y. That's a good choice, too. But for the sake of comparison, it's easier to focus on one model, so I'm going with the iPhone.

Okay then, let's begin with the conclusion!

Drum roll … da-da-da-da-dah … The most efficient and inexpensive way to own and operate an iPhone is to buy a new SIM-free model from an Apple Store, not a telecommunications provider, and choose the cheapest possible SIM card from a company, which matches your monthly gigabyte usage and call needs.

'What – is that all?' I hear you say. I know it might sound counter-intuitive, with all the tempting plans available from various providers, but after repeated calculations I can tell you that this appears to be the most efficient and economical way. Here's why.

Currently the latest 16GB iPhone costs ¥66,744 (including tax). Divide this by 24 for a per-monthly cost of ¥2,781. Then add the SIM cost. A SIM card with unlimited usage will set you back about ¥3,000 per month, so even if you are constantly using Wi-Fi, the total monthly cost still comes to slightly less than ¥6,000. I chose this option because I don't have Wi-Fi at home, but there are many cheaper SIMs available if that's not a consideration.

You will save over ¥2,000 a month doing it like this, compared with buying a new iPhone from a certain Company D for two years with 5GHz Wi-Fi usage for ¥8,000 a month. That will actually end up costing more because it doesn't include the phone bill.

If you decide to go with a smartphone bought directly from Apple for four years instead of two, then the monthly cost is even lower. This is why it's good to buy the latest model. None of the low-cost smartphone companies still offers the iPhone 7. If you intend using your smartphone for a long time, buying a new one from Apple is the better deal.

Something else to think about is the fact that cheap SIM cards often have short or no minimum usage periods. Some companies will allow you to switch to another provider and keep your number after a few months, six months, a year, or even a month (although there are administrative fees involved). If you find a company with better terms, you can keep switching.

If you buy a smartphone direct from Apple you can also use it overseas. Just buy a disposable SIM card locally and insert it.

It was late. Sunday had turned into Monday, and when the sun rose, a new week would begin. But Miho was not yet sleepy, and kept tapping away at her computer.

Miho had started her blog the same day she attended Suko Kurofune's seminar. It was a suggestion from her sister that had set her off. Her efforts at economising hadn't been producing great results, and with the setbacks she soon encountered, seemed to be wasting money instead of saving it. On days when she had been working late and was tired, she often felt the urge to buy things. Gourmet bread from an upscale bakery that was open until ten at night, or dessert from the shelf of a convenience store if it was any later. This habit was something she'd become aware of after she started keeping a record of her spending in her daily schedule. She hadn't been confident of being able to keep up with the entries in a special-purpose kakeibō, so Maho had suggested writing down just a few things in a notebook instead. Even doing just this would make a difference, she'd insisted.

Miho had been thinking for some time that a blog might be one way to help keep herself on track with economising. Having even just a few readers would be incentive to stick with it. Then, after being inspired by Suko Kurofune, she decided to channel this feeling into action straight away.

I went to a seminar marking the publication of 8 x 12 Is the Magic Number *by Suko Kurofune!*

She knew what she wanted to say and had no trouble finding topics for her posts. Writing under a pseudonym, she called her blog *Economising with Peanut: My Goal Is to Buy a House and Adopt a Rescue Dog.*

At the same time, she created a new Twitter account with the handle Peanut @economisingblogger to tweet updates to her blog. Ms Kurofune had come across it and introduced Miho's blog to her own tens of thousands of followers:

'Here's a good summary of my seminar on *8 x 12 Is the Magic Number* at a bookstore the other day. Thank you, Peanut.'

Miho was most grateful, and thanks to this tweet her blog got off to a good start, with page views of the seminar report soaring to four digits. The day before, on only her third day of blogging, she was already running out of material. Then she recalled something her grandmother had said, and put together a post with the title *How You Use Three Thousand Yen*

Can Decide Your Life (maybe). Miho wrote about her grandmother's observations on teapots – the kind her mother and sister used – and how it bothered her that she had yet to find a teapot for herself that was just right. This post also attracted many views, and Miho decided to do occasional posts about her family's efforts at economising, as well as her own.

Her frank account of losing Peanut, and how she had started saving to buy a house where she could keep a rescue dog, was another popular post, attracting many comments: 'I know how you feel. My dog died too and I cried when I read this.' Slowly but steadily, her readers were increasing.

Ten months after they had met, just as her birthday was approaching, Miho received a message from Shohei saying he needed to talk. The pair had not made any formal betrothal, or exchanged rings, but they spoke to each other as if it were an established fact that they planned to marry. Shohei had brought up marriage right from the beginning of their relationship. After only a few dates, he started casually dropping topics such as his ideal family into conversation, and how many children he wanted. After her experience with her previous boyfriend, Daiki, who stopped mentioning anything of the kind once he started work, Miho found this both refreshing and gratifying.

When she asked Shohei why he was so keen to get married, he replied earnestly that he wanted to start his own family and settle down as soon as possible. Miho probed further, to find out whether his reason for wanting a family so much was due to a particularly positive image of family life, or because there had been problems with his own. Shohei responded by saying, 'I can't put it very well.'

'Why not?'

'It's not like there was any abuse or problems as such, just that my family was . . .' Shohei's eyes went distant as he thought, '. . . loose.'

'Loose?'

'Yeah. Nothing specific, just that home was kind of loose, and slack – not substantial. Well, that's how I feel now, but I didn't understand it at the time.'

'What are your mother and father like?'

'They're both normal, kind people. Not violent or abusive, but still . . . I couldn't really say what they're like. We almost never talked properly about anything serious. My father quit his job when I was in high school apparently, but I'm not really sure what happened with that either. When I told him I wanted to go to art college, he wasn't for or against it. I asked my mother if she was sure it was okay for me to go, because tuition is really expensive, you know, and she just laughed and said, "Don't be so heavy." She always says that. "Don't be so heavy."'

Miho was surprised that his mother would use such a slangy expression, but she assumed that Shohei's family was one where the parents were like friends. And she had heard even her own mother say jokingly, 'That's heavy!' before.

The town where Shohei's parents lived was further east than Jujo, on the border of Saitama Prefecture. Shohei had lived at home until finishing art school, then moved into a flat on his own in Akabane when he got the internship.

Miho was in no doubt about her feelings for Shohei, and had no reservations when he suddenly said, 'I want to get married.' Their mutual attraction seemed to deepen with every meeting. She was puzzled, then, by his message. *What does he need to talk about now?* she wondered, while waiting for him in a fast-food restaurant near Jujo Station early in the morning. *Does he want to know where I want to go for my birthday?* In the early days of their relationship, when Shohei was a new intern, it had been much easier to find time to meet. Now, it was almost impossible on weekdays. Even using her flexitime, Miho still had to be at work by 10 a.m., while Shohei's company started their day before noon and worked through until late into the night. The upshot was when they really wanted to see each other on a weekday, they mostly did breakfast dates, and would chat over a cheap breakfast set menu.

'I thought about waiting till the weekend to talk but decided it was best to tell you as soon as possible.' Shohei had been doing late nights because of an impending work deadline at the end of the month, and his eyes were red.

'What's up? Why couldn't you message?'

'I have to tell you in person. It's really important.'

'What could be so important?'

'Yesterday I had a phone call from an organisation I'd never heard of before.'

'Who?

'They said that I was behind on my student loan repayments.'

'What? You had a student loan?' This was news to Miho.

'I had no idea. My parents applied for it without telling me. They filled out the forms too.'

Miho said nothing.

'When I asked them about it, they told me they'd taken out a student loan to pay my tuition. They paid back some while I was still at uni, but now I'm working they told me to pay back the rest myself.'

Questions crowded into Miho's mind. 'But didn't you tell me that you gave them money from your part-time job to pay for tuition and living expenses? And you funded the overseas study yourself through the part-time job, right?' She remembered this well because of the impression it had given her, of what a solid and dependable guy Shohei was.

'Yes, I did. I gave them fifty thousand yen every month for living expenses, housing and tuition. But they told me it was nowhere near enough. And tuition fees at art school are steep.'

Shohei's parents certainly did have a point. Still . . .

'How much is it? The loan?' Miho asked, trying for a casual note. She didn't want to be overly dramatic about this, but she was aware that her voice was faltering.

'In total they borrowed one hundred and twenty thousand yen every month.'

'What? One hundred and twenty thousand . . .'

'It was interest-free while I was still a student, but now I've graduated a three per cent interest charge applies. Without interest, the full sum was 5.76 million yen. But since they repaid some, it's now 5.5 million. Of course I can't pay it back all at once, so I'll have to repay it, little by little.'

Miho felt numb. She almost stopped breathing, and couldn't speak.

'I'm so sorry to spring this on you.' Shohei bowed his head in apology.

At the sight, her emotions returned. 'It's not your fault.' But when she tried to think whose fault it was, she was still not satisfied. 'So, it's you who has to repay it, then?'

'Why do you say that?' Shohei looked at her directly.

'Because you're being forced into repaying a loan you didn't even know about. I mean, you didn't fill in the forms, right?'

He shook his head. 'I thought about that, too. I didn't know about the loan, and the signature is my parents' handwriting. They thought that if they just paid back what they could, things would somehow be all right. But the fact is that money was spent on me. For me to study at art school, as I dreamed. There's no getting away from that. And thanks to that education, I landed my job at a design firm.'

True, thought Miho, *but he works extremely hard for very little pay.*

'That's why I can't just ignore it. It'll come back to me anyway, if my parents die still owing that debt.'

'But the loan was one hundred and twenty thousand yen a month, and you also paid fifty thousand each month, right? One hundred and seventy thousand by twelve comes to over two million a year. Was art college really that expensive?'

'Tuition was around 1.5 million. And then there's food and accommodation as well.'

Couldn't his parents at least have borne those costs while he was still a dependant? But Miho kept that thought to herself.

'I don't know what to say. I only just heard about this myself. I'm still not sure how I feel.'

Miho reminded herself that Shohei would have had the biggest shock. She remembered what he had said before about his parents being 'loose'. What were they like? For Miho, parents were people who surrounded and protected you. She was sometimes angry with her own, and they quarrelled, and her father could be frustrating because he never showed much emotion, but never had they given her cause for concern the way Shohei's were. Had they been violent or abusive it might have been easier to think of them as terrible parents, but in this situation, she didn't know what to think.

Miho tried to picture them, but came up blank. They didn't sound like any of her friends' parents, and she found it impossible to conjure up an image of them. But she could imagine a sneer on those blank faces.

I should talk to Maho. She knows about interest rates and stuff. With a start, Miho realised the direction her thoughts were taking.

'Oh dear . . .' Miho's mother, Tomoko, frowned deeply and fell silent.

Miho, Tomoko, Maho and their grandmother, Kotoko, were all gathered in the living room of the Mikuriya family home. Kotoko, who could usually be relied on to cheerfully smooth things over, was also silent.

A few days earlier, Miho had phoned Maho for advice about Shohei's loan.

'This is not good,' Maho had immediately said. 'With a sum that large, I couldn't judge on my own.' She recommended Miho talk to their parents. It just so happened that on Friday, a day when Taiyo was working the night shift, Maho was taking Saho over to her parents' house for dinner, so she suggested Miho go, too. Their father had drinks after work but would be home before ten.

However, uncomfortable at the idea of discussing her boyfriend and his money problems with just her mother and sister, Miho decided to ask her grandmother to join them. Lately her mother was quick to become emotional, which Miho put down to menopause, and she was counting on her grandmother to keep her mother in check.

'Does he know exactly how he's going to pay off this debt?' Maho asked, taking the role of mediator, but in a stern tone nonetheless.

'It's not a debt, it's a student loan.'

'Same thing, isn't it?'

'I think it's different, but . . . Anyway, he talked to the association that lent the money, and he's supposed to repay about thirty thousand every month.'

'Did you ask *exactly* how much? Not just *about*? You need to be clear on that,' Maho insisted, whipping out her smartphone to open the calculator app.

Miho checked the figures she had noted down on her smartphone memo after hearing them from Shohei. 'Probably about 30,500 yen.'

'Assuming the loan is for 5.5 million yen. Pay back 30,500 yen a month at three per cent interest,' she mumbled, tapping on the calculator. '. . . twenty years. I calculate it will take exactly twenty years to repay.'

'Twenty years? That long?'

'The interest alone is 182,795 yen! They might have only

borrowed 5.5 million, but the actual amount they will eventually have to return comes to 7,320,795 yen in total.'

'Thirty thousand every month for twenty years is a lot of money, you know. . . .' Tomoko spoke as if with great effort.

I know. More than anybody, I know that, thought Miho. Not so long ago she had moved to Jujo and begun trying to save money. She had reviewed her fixed costs – rent, smartphone, life insurance and so on – and started taking her own lunch to work. Finally, she was at a point now where saving ¥40,000 each month was within reach. Yes, she was well aware of what a substantial sum ¥30,000 a month was.

'I am against any marriage,' her mother finally looked up and said flatly.

'What?'

Miho had been preparing herself for the possibility that she might encounter resistance, but had not expected her mother to come out so definitively. She had always been the golden girl in the Mikuriya family, attending the top high school in their school district and going to the university of her choice. Almost never had her parents been angry with her or opposed any of her decisions.

'Even though I don't know what he's like because I've never met him,' added Tomoko.

'Then you should meet him,' murmured Miho.

Curtly, her mother shook her head. 'I'm sure he's very nice. He must be if you chose him, Miho. And naturally that's why I can't tell you to break off with him. But I do want you to postpone any idea of marriage for a while. Go out with him a bit longer, and then give the matter some good thought.'

Though couched in roundabout terms, Miho could tell this was a resounding no.

'But the loan wasn't his fault. Shohei didn't even know about it.'

'There's no need to rush into anything now. Why not take some time to think more, as your mother suggests? You're not planning to marry soon, are you, Miho?' Kotoko finally chimed in. 'How about I meet him? On the understanding that we are on a wait-and-see basis. Bring him over to my house and I can at least get some idea of what kind of young man he is.'

'I'd be happy to introduce him to you, Grandma. You'll see he's really kind and intelligent.'

'Excuse me. Please don't interfere, Mother,' Tomoko said heatedly. It was a rare thing for her to defy her mother-in-law.

'Tomoko?'

'If you meet him, he may get the impression that this relationship has the blessing of the family, which is not the case. We still cannot give our assent to any marriage.'

Miho had never heard her mother oppose her grandmother in such outright terms before. That alone made her even more keenly aware of the enormity and responsibility a debt of this size entailed.

'I wasn't planning on saying this,' Miho's mother sighed. 'But I will now so that you may understand, too, Mother. It's not just the money issue that worries me. If Miho marries this boy she will have a familial connection with her in-laws. But to be clear, I have to wonder what kind of people would borrow a full student loan without telling their son, and then force him into paying it back once it's started accruing interest.'

'But Miho is marrying him, not the parents,' Maho interjected.

Miho observed her mother glare at Maho. 'Married life is a very long time. And you can never know what the future will be. We cannot gloss over that reality by talking about it as if the family doesn't matter, or everything will be fine, because the partner is a good person. Japan is not the kind of society where things can be that simple. You're married, too, Maho, so you should know.'

'Yes, that's for sure . . .'

The doorbell chimed, announcing her father's return. Tomoko rose and went to let him in.

'It wasn't so uncommon in the past for married couples to have that kind of debt,' Kotoko murmured quietly, looking in the direction of the front door.

'Chin up,' Maho said, patting Miho on the back. 'I have a friend whose fiancé's parents put a one hundred million yen life insurance policy on her.'

I must look pretty down if Maho feels she has to pull out a story like that to console me, Miho thought. 'What happened to her?' she asked.

'She discussed it with her fiancé, but wasn't satisfied with his answer and broke off the engagement in the end.'

Miho was hardly comforted.

'I'm home.'

Miho's father entered the room and met her eyes. His expression was the same as always, in spite of the fact that she was certain her mother would have given him a quick rundown of the situation.

'Welcome home,' the three women said in unison.

Miho's mother still looked grim.

'I'll just get changed,' her father said, and quickly went into the bedroom.

'Miho, you have to tell your father everything.'

'I know.'

While her father was changing, her mother put his dinner on the table. He reappeared dressed in a sweatshirt and track pants. Miho quickly explained the situation as he ate, while her sister and grandmother listened, with bated breath, from the living room.

'I can say nothing to you,' he said.

'What?' Miho's mother was the first to react.

'How can I object? You like this boy, don't you, Miho? Talk it over with your mother,' he said blandly, continuing to eat.

'Oh, you are so ...' Tomoko held her head in her hands. 'You always do this! Wriggle out of everything and play nice!'

'Mum, I don't think that's what he's doing.'

'It's always me who's left to be the mean one. Because I'm the opposite of whatever he says.' Tomoko stood up and went to her room. She banged the door shut.

Miho's father watched her open-mouthed. *Don't make a face like that, why don't you just say what you think?* Miho thought crossly. She couldn't be bothered with her parents at this moment, and looked over to her grandmother and Maho.

'What should I do?'

'You have to have a proper discussion with your father and

mother,' Kotoko said firmly. 'They are your parents, and they worry. There's no getting around it – seven million yen is a lot of money.'

'Five point five million.'

'Yes, but . . .' Kotoko turned to her son, Miho's father. 'You need to have a proper talk with Tomoko.'

'Yep,' he grunted, already back to eating his meal.

Miho looked at Maho, who shrugged her shoulders. Was she saying *I don't want to get involved* or *It's up to you to decide*? Miho couldn't tell.

Jujo was nothing fancy, but the town where Shohei had grown up was even less so. Everything was in plain sight there. This was not something that should have escaped Miho's notice. She had seen the late-night TV programmes in recent years where it was featured as a town that never sleeps, with rows of bars open until the early hours of the morning, and during the day as well, and a small red-light district behind the station. She had also read in magazines about the many cheap bars where you could get dead drunk for only ¥1,000. The thought had crossed her mind that she would like to see it once, but going there for the purpose of meeting her fiancé's parents? That was different.

A few days earlier, Miho and Shohei had been talking over the student loan yet again, when apprehensively she had asked, 'What kind of people are your parents?' The student-loan issue would be awkward, but her desire to meet his parents took precedence. Shohei immediately invited her to visit.

Miho was nervous when they alighted from the train. His family lived a ten-minute walk from the station in a rented house, and on the way there they passed through the main street full of bars before coming to one lined with wooden houses and flats.

'Kanako, I'm home!' Shohei suddenly shouted, banging on the sliding front door of a wooden house. Miho jumped at the loud, resounding knocks.

'Who's Kanako?'

'Ma, my mother,' Shohei replied as simultaneously the door opened. A middle-aged woman holding a small dog stood grinning at them.

'Welcome home.'

'I brought a friend with me.'

Shohei's mother gave Miho a searching look. 'Friend? Girlfriend more like it?'

Kanako was wearing a pink knitwear top and denim jeans, which wouldn't have looked strange on a woman in her twenties, but still suited Kanako, with her brown-dyed hair.

'Er, nice to meet you, I'm Miho Mikuriya.' Miho bowed so deeply her head almost touched the ground.

'I've heard about you. From Sho. The place is a mess, but please come in.'

Miho was relieved that Shohei's mother seemed warmer and more ordinary than expected. Piles of old magazines and plastic storage boxes filled with clothes lined the corridor leading from the front door to the living room.

'Can't you tidy up when people come over?' Shohei complained to his mother.

'Well, you did spring this on me.'

'Ah, sorry. But it's okay. Wouldn't have made any difference even if I did give you more warning.' Shohei laughed.

The eight-tatami-mat-sized living room, approximately three and a half square metres, was filled with large pieces of furniture: two sofas, a table and two televisions side by side. A man, who Miho assumed must be Shohei's brother, was playing a video game on one TV and occupying one sofa, while his father sat on the other sofa watching live golf on the other TV. Both were on the heavy side and looked a lot alike. Shohei resembled his mother more, Miho decided.

Shohei had two older brothers. The eldest worked for a local construction company and still lived at home, while the middle son was married and apparently rarely ever visited.

With both sofas occupied, Miho remained standing beside them.

'Hey, you two, one of you move over! There's nowhere for Shohei's girlfriend to sit!' Kanako shouted.

Shohei's father stood up obediently and moved next to the brother. Neither of them gave Miho barely a glance. She had been thinking that she ought to introduce herself, or at least give her name, but couldn't find the right moment.

'Sit wherever you can find space,' Kanako said.

At this, Miho sat herself down in the place Shohei's father had vacated. It still felt uncomfortably warm from his body.

Kanako brought in tea for Miho, Shohei and herself. Miho thanked her and took a sip, but since the father and brother were served nothing, she felt rude about drinking more.

The family continued to watch TV, saying nothing to each other.

Suddenly, the father turned towards Miho. 'You play golf?'

'Me?' she said, startled, pointing at herself.'

'Yeah.'

'Er, no I don't. My father does, though.'

'Humph.'

Again, there was silence.

'Um, do you play golf?' Miho asked, unable to stand it anymore.

'Me?' the father asked.

'Er, yes.'

'Nope.' And he laughed.

'Eita's into bikes,' Shohei informed her.

'Bikes?'

'Eita rides motorbikes,' Kanako explained.

Miho was finally catching on that in this family the parents were called by their first names. She hadn't realised this before as Shohei always referred to them as his mother and father.

'Oh, I see ... do you often go for rides?'

'Nope. Put on weight, he has. Doesn't ride much now. Gets tired. And he's getting on. But recently, he bought a new motorbike with a two-million-yen loan. Even though he doesn't ride much.'

For some reason, everyone except Miho guffawed.

'That's not good,' Shohei warned him laughingly.

'Don't be so heavy,' Miho heard Kanako say, just as Shohei had said.

When dinner time approached, Shohei stood up and said, 'Well, we'll go now and get something to eat.'

'Oh, okay.'

Nobody tried to stop them and only Kanako saw them to the door. Shohei's brother continued to play his game the whole time they were there without once making eye contact.

'Um, did I . . .' Miho tentatively began as they walked to the station.

'Did you what?

'Did I do something wrong?'

'Why? What?'

'I wondered if I made some kind of faux pas?'

'Huh?'

Miho looked at Shohei, who appeared completely mystified by her question. She decided not to pursue it. *That's the kind of family they are.* There had been no greetings, no introductions, no conversation, no invitation to dinner, and the only hospitality offered was a cup of tea, but that didn't mean they disliked her, or harboured her any ill will. Maybe. They just seemed like people who did not care so much about loans.

On the other hand, she could understand why Shohei could not be hard-hearted towards his family, or cut them off. They weren't such bad people that he could do that to them. They just hadn't grown up. Maybe growing up in this environment was what had enabled Shohei to hone his artistic talent.

Shohei and Miho found a cheap *izakaya* near the station where the bill for food and drink truly did cost less than ¥3,000 for two, then Miho went back to Jujo.

What am I going to do? she thought on the return journey. *What should I do now?*

Rather than write about something that happened, or my thoughts on anything, today I want to ask your advice.

What would you do if your fiancé told you something shocking? Something that could be a major obstacle to your relationship and marriage? Something that is not his fault, but his relatives'? But now my own parents know about this something, they strongly oppose us getting married.

The thing is, if we do get married, I will have to postpone my goal of buying a house and adopting a rescue dog for a very long time. That's how major this something is. What would you do?

Miho was overcome by nostalgia at the sight of Machie outside Asagaya Station in her brown cardigan and brown skirt – the same outfit as she always wore.

'Hello, Miho, it's been so long. I was delighted when you wrote and said you wanted to meet.' Machie took Miho's hand and clasped it with a smile. 'I'm so sorry to make you come all the way to Asagaya. But Mother is not too well and I can't leave the house for very long, which is not really in any state for receiving visitors, anyway.'

'Is your mother ill?'

'I think the move might not have been very good for her heart. She took a sudden turn for the worse around the end of last year. But she's fine if she stays at home and rests.'

They entered a coffee shop near the station and began to talk. Miho had learned in an email a week earlier that Machie and her mother had moved out of their big house. They were now living in a rented flat close to Asagaya Station.

'Oh, so what happened to the house?'

'We sold it.'

'Oh.'

'But it was for the best. A local real-estate agent had been offering for a long time to buy the property. They're going to demolish the house and build a small block of flats on the site. Mother and I will live in one. Meanwhile, we have temporary accommodation elsewhere.'

Though Machie had lost some weight, her colour was better and she seemed rejuvenated. She'd changed her hairstyle too, with a part in the fringe that showed her forehead.

'It was a hard decision, since we were both very attached to the house, especially Mother, but my resigning was a good opportunity.'

Machie didn't mention it of course, but Miho could imagine that they must have received a significant amount of money, too.

'I rather like where we're living now, which is very close to the station. It's much smaller than the old place, but warmer, and the bathroom is lovely. I also only need one key to lock up when I go out, which is a blessing. Even Mother says, "Machie, we should have moved sooner."'

'Is that right. Um, what about work?'

'Oh, it's nothing special. I'm studying how to be a carer. After all, Mother will obviously need it someday, and at my age, I had limited options as to the kind of work I could start doing.'

'I don't think being a carer is nothing special. It's fine work.'

'When Mother picks up a little, I plan to find a part-time job at a facility to begin with. Then I want to study to become an administrative scrivener if possible. That means I can undertake to be an adult guardian. And if I qualify as a care manager as well, I should have no problem finding work, apparently.'

Aha, this is why Machie is looking brighter. She's found a goal in life. It wasn't just moving or selling the house for a lot of money that did it.

'What about you, Miho? Is there something you wanted to talk about?'

'Actually . . .' Miho hesitated, wondering where to begin. 'Actually, I'm seeing someone right now.'

'I see.'

'And he says he wants to marry me, but . . .' Miho told her about Shohei's student loan. Machie listened intently.

'Five and a half million yen is certainly a lot of money.' Machie was silent for a while.

Everyone has the same reaction. 'It's just a student loan,' they say at first, but hearing the actual amount shuts them up.

'You know, leaving the company taught me something,' Machie said, eventually, looking up. 'I learned that there are opportunities at any stage in life. I worked in the same job for over twenty years, and thought that my life was over when I left, but it wasn't.'

'It wasn't?'

'In this day and age, there's no such thing.'

'You really think so?

'I know that everybody should be prepared to start over again, at any time. That applies, whether you have debts or not.'

The old Machie had always been a kind and good person, but now she also seems a little wiser, thought Miho.

Today I met a former senior colleague from work. She left her job for various reasons and is now studying to be a carer and qualify as a notary public at the same time, with the idea of becoming a care manager in future. According to her, she may not have any skills right now, but if she starts studying while working at a facility (where apparently it is relatively easy to get work), and qualifies as an administrative scrivener and care manager, she will never go hungry.

I was hugely encouraged to hear her. It made me realise that you can always start over from scratch, even when you lose everything. I've been feeling down ever since my boyfriend told me about his student loan, but seeing my old colleague today made me feel better. I love my job. It's fulfilling, and I get on well with the people I work with. I also want to keep up this blog.

I'll be straight with you. The truth is, my boyfriend has a ¥5.5 million debt from a student loan. His parents signed up for it on his behalf and borrowed the money without his knowledge. If I marry him, we will have to pay back over ¥30,000 every month for the next twenty years. We can do it if we both work hard, but it will mean giving up any other plans for anything else we might be able to do with that money. Say we repay the debt in twenty years. I will be in my mid-forties by then, and we'll be virtually starting from zero. I love my boyfriend, but when I think about this it scares me a bit.

If I get married, of course I want to have children and buy a house, too. These are modest dreams, but will they be possible? I honestly don't know what to do.

The day after posting this, Miho received a call from Shohei. A voice call, no video.

'I read your post,' he said, sounding tired, then went silent.

'Sorry,' Miho eventually replied, though she didn't know why she was apologising.

'It's okay. Your reaction is normal. It's natural that you're worried. I got a shock myself.'

'Yeah.'

'I'm glad to know what you honestly think.'

'Yeah.'

'But I was a bit sad.' Shohei laughed in a way that sounded like bravado to Miho's ears. 'I guess I was hoping maybe you wouldn't care too much.'

'You were hoping? For what?'

'Oh, hoping you might be positive and say "let's pay it back together" or something.'

'I thought that you were the one who didn't seem to care so much.'

'About what?'

'The debt – er, I mean student loan.'

'I do care. How can I not?'

'Oh? It doesn't look like way.'

'What do you mean *look that way*?'

Miho hesitated. She knew she had to explain herself properly. 'When I met your parents, they didn't mention the student loan at all. I couldn't bring it up either ... but I was kind of hoping that maybe you would, and ask your parents what their thoughts were, or how they felt about it.'

'Nah, I couldn't do that – you saw what my family's like.'

'Yeah, I did. And they mentioned the motorbike debt, too. I could see your family don't worry so much about that kind of thing. That's why I was having trouble seeing the future.' Miho didn't feel she could say anything more critical of Shohei's parents.

'I was going to bring it up for discussion with them in due course.'

'I don't know about that.'

'What?'

'Bring it up in due course ... This kind of thing – really? I know that someone has to repay the debt. But I think there's not much chance that your parents could say anything that would satisfy me.'

'It ... it might be a tall order.'

'Right.' Miho knew already, without asking Shohei, that they would have to repay the money. 'So it's not about that, or hoping what other people will do, but what you and I are going to do. How are *we* going to deal with it? The situation won't change, so, maybe, it comes down to how am I going to come to terms with it?'

What she thought, but did not say aloud was, *In the end it's down to me. How am I going to fit that 5.5 million-yen debt into my life plan?*

'I think I get what you're saying, Miho.'

'Do you?'

'I think you're saying we need to put some space between us, and each think about it.'

Miho made a startled sound but said nothing more, because in her heart of hearts, she *had* been thinking this.

'After reading your blog, I got it. I can't force you to do anything or get you involved. So, I won't contact you for a while. If you want to talk, send a message or email.'

No, that's not true, she wanted to say, *I don't mind being involved if it's with you.* But in this moment, those words didn't feel like the right ones to express her feelings, either, so she said nothing.

'Bye, Miho. Take care,' Shohei said gently. He hung up before he could hear her reply, 'I know you're busy, but you take care, too.'

Seeing as Respect-for-Senior-Citizens Day is coming up soon, I wanted to tell you about my grandmother, who I'll call Funeko.

Some of you told me when I mentioned Funeko before, that she sounds interesting, and cheers you up, so I decided to ask her, if she was going to write a blog, what she would write about. She gave me a range of suggestions. For example: Why I Looked for Work at the Age of Seventy-Three, How to Make Super Fast and Easy Fermented Rice Bran for Pickling *and* The Day of the 26 February Incident as Heard from My Mother. *Catchy, aren't they? But I decided to go with one about gardening. I think this will interest my readers, and it's also what my grandmother does best. So here's today's post:*

Hundred-Yen Gardening.

Have you ever thought that it might be nice to have a bit of green inside the house, but you didn't know where to start? Maybe you've had inside pot plants that died. When I thought about what kind of plant would be suitable for a young single woman living on her own, I decided it should be something easy to look after, attractive and easy on the pocket. Here's what you can do.

First, visit a 100-yen shop. Buy some potting soil and the biggest plastic pot you can find. The bigger the better. Any shape will do. A planter is fine, too. Take it home and fill the pot with the soil. Cover the water-drainage hole in the bottom with some net or mesh. Like the mesh bag that you buy oranges in. Next, go to the supermarket and buy some spring onions, mitsuba and coriander (if you like). Or choose your favourite herb or vegetable. But it must have roots. That's the only thing you need to make sure of.

Plants that you use for garnishes are good because you only use a little at a time, and there is usually too much left over when you buy bunches of them. Especially if you live alone or with a small family. But it's very convenient to have them growing at home, to use a little at a time whenever you need.

Buy your plant and cut it off about 5cm above the root. Don't forget to use the leaves for cooking. (If you can't use them all, chop up finely and put in the freezer.) Then soak the roots in a glass of water for a day or two, drain and plant in the pot. You don't need to buy a trowel or any kind of gardening tool. Just make a hole in the soil with chopsticks and insert the plant.

You can make a bed of different plants in the one pot, arranging them according to height. For example, put spring onions at the back, with mitsuba or coriander in front. If you prefer shiso or parsley to coriander, you can buy seedlings from a garden shop (these are also only about ¥100). In this way, leftover herbs from the kitchen can be turned into an indoor bed of greenery.

Once you've planted the roots, water them until it flows from the bottom. In a month or so, you will be able to harvest. If you pick and use a little of each plant at a time, the shoots will have a chance to sprout again.

Here, Miho pasted a photograph of a herb bed in a pot that her grandmother had made. The spring onions grew tall and straight, complemented by the smaller *mitsuba* and parsley growing thick in front, and just as Kotoko had said it would, it added a lovely touch of green.

'Are you sure this kind of thing is all right?' Funeko, aka Miho's grandmother Kotoko, peered anxiously at Miho's screen. 'Everyone does it, don't they?' she said.

'No, I told you they don't.'

While Miho tidied up the formatting, Kotoko made a pot of fragrant tea in her lovely teapot.

'This is delicious, Grandma.'

'It's Darjeeling. I buy it in small quantities at speciality stores. I always measure it out properly with a teaspoon, use freshly boiled water and put a tea cosy on the pot.'

The soft and fluffy tea cosy, handsewn from quilted cloth, lay next to the pot.

'Speaking of days off, why aren't you with Shohei today? Did anything happen?'

Kotoko apparently had read Miho's last post. After Miho had told her about the blog site, she bookmarked it in her smartphone and read it from time to time.

'Uh-huh.'

'Over money?'

'When I wrote about the ... student loan, I got quite a reaction.'

In fact, it was more than 'quite a reaction'. Two days later a well-known blogger and author tweeted a comment about her post: 'This woman is worried about her fiancé's student loan. I'd like to encourage her but 5.5 million is a huge debt. Something needs to be done about this system.' She linked Miho's post to her comment.

This was retweeted by various bloggers in turn, while others quoted it and added their opinion before retweeting as well. The page view count on Miho's post shot up to five figures, and the number of reader comments increased by an order of magnitude. Not all were favourable, however. While many wished her 'good luck', with sympathetic comments such as 'I know how you feel. It's hard to know what to do,' others were harsh: 'This person is not qualified to marry,' 'You're starting from the wrong assumption. If money is so important, look for a rich guy to begin with,' 'I feel sorry for your boyfriend that you wrote this' and, 'Not wanting to repay borrowed money is the same as being a thief.'

Miho became depressed, and even a little scared. Some comments completely twisted what she'd written. It was not an easy thing to explain your feelings to so many people, she realised.

Very soon, she wrote another post. *Thank you very much for everyone's input. I will have a quiet think about all of this.* Despite everything, she was still keen to continue the blog, hence her invitation to Kotoko to make an appearance.

'Isn't there something more important than your blog?'

'What?'

'Shohei. Did you talk to your parents again after last time?'

'No, but I met Shohei's family.'

Miho gave Kotoko a rundown of the visit to Shohei's parents, telling her about her surprise at how different their ideas about debt seemed to be compared to her own parents, and the other debts that the family appeared to have, along with her sense that at bottom they weren't bad people.

'I see.'

'What do you think, Grandma? What would you do?'

'It's a difficult one,' Kotoko hedged.

'You said before, that it used to be common for people to have that much debt.'

'Well, yes, but the cost of living was different then, too. Once upon a time when prices rose, salaries would also rise, and if you kept your nose to the grindstone it was possible to repay a debt after ten years or so by chipping away at it. But now, well, the economy may doing a little better, but if deflation sets in any debt will effectively increase.'

'Don't scare me.'

Kotoko shook her head. 'I wasn't trying to. Besides, it's true what Maho said, that you're marrying Shohei and not his parents. If he's solid then you're fine. Good men are rare.'

'I wonder if he is.'

'If he's a good worker, isn't violent, and doesn't gamble or drink too much, that might be enough.'

Kotoko went on to tell Miho about a job-hopper she knew called Yasuo, and a writer called Kinari, who had recently started living together.

'Yasuo doesn't make much money, but Kinari still thinks he's all right.'

'What's so good about him?'

'She probably prefers a chance at making a family and life together with him more than money.'

'I see.'

'The point is, ultimately, it's up to you, Miho. You're the one who has to take responsibility for your life. No matter how hard your parents or I try to do our best for you, we can't live your life for you.'

This was no solace to Miho, who found these words terrifying.

Miho had not spoken with Shohei in several weeks when she received an email from him. Her heart leaped when his name popped up in her inbox, but this was quickly followed by disappointment when she realised it was a mass mailing.

> I have just completed my first solo project in my new job. It was a commission for a poster advertising the concert schedule of the European classical music duo, *Favourite*. Posters will be on display at all major JR stations from the first of next month, but stations near concert halls, like Ueno, Roppongi and Shibuya, are your best bet of spotting it. If you have a chance, please take a moment to stop and look at my work.

Miho had an idea, and immediately called Kotoko. 'Grandma, remember you said before that you would meet Shohei?

Well, how about coming with me to see a poster he designed instead?'

Miho herself had never seen one of his posters before. But she had seen the graphic design on his graduation project and was confident it would be good.

'That's very nice of you, Miho dear, but you really ought to ask your mother and father.'

'What? No way would they go. They're totally against Shohei.'

'That's not true. You're their precious daughter, so of course they want to know more about him. If your mother won't go, then I will.'

'But . . .'

'This is between you and your parents.'

Miho had not been in contact with her mother since the discussion about marriage that day, and still felt awkward. She sent a brief email laying out the facts: *A poster that Shohei designed will be on display at JR stations. I'm going to see it on the first and wondered if you would like to go with me.*

Two days went by, and Miho had almost given up, when she received a reply: *Yes, I'll go.*

On the morning of the first, Miho kept an eye out for the poster on her daily commute from Jujo, but she did not spot it. After work she went to meet her mother outside the ticket gate near the Hachiko exit of Shibuya Station, and found her mother with a tight-lipped expression, standing next to her father.

'Hey, you came, too, Dad?'

'He said he wanted to see this poster when I told him about it.'

Miho looked at her father, and he nodded. 'It's important.'

She was surprised to hear him say this.

'It's important to you, Miho – isn't it?' he persisted.

Not sure of how to answer, Miho said nothing.

'Well, let's go and look for it,' said her mother.

They walked around the JR side of the station first, searching for the poster.

'Mum, are you okay?' asked Miho, concerned because of her mother's recent surgery.

Her question drew a faint smile at last from Tomoko. 'I'm fine to go walking now. A certain amount of exercise is good, apparently, to prevent the internal cut from fusing.'

'Recently we've been going out for walks on my days off,' Miho's father added quietly.

'Wow.' They'd never done anything like that when Miho lived at home. She couldn't imagine it. Perhaps their lives had changed now that they were on their own.

'Surprisingly, your father likes to walk and is quite fast. The golf must keep him in shape.'

Was it her imagination, Miho wondered, that her mother sounded slightly shy?

They trudged along outside the station in the direction of the Tokyu department store without finding any likely candidates for Shohei's work. Whenever there was a concert poster, Miho would run ahead to check while her parents followed more slowly behind. She felt as if she had regressed to childhood. But rarely had she and her parents gone out on their own, as being the second daughter, her sister Maho was always with them. The only time that she could recall it being only the three of them together was at her university graduation ceremony.

Oh, but there was one time. Miho suddenly remembered her grade two sports day, when Maho caught the flu. She had had to stay at their grandmother's house while the other three went to the sports day. On the way home, Miho, her father and mother had walked side by side, all holding hands. As much as Miho was close to Maho, and cared about her sister, she was always longing for more of her parents' attention and was thrilled to have them to herself that day. She skipped along excitedly between her father and mother, feeling so happy that her feet barely touched the ground and she nearly took a tumble several times. Thinking back on it now, she felt tenderly protective of her younger self.

It also surprised her to realise that despite her impression of her father's aloofness from family matters, he had in fact always attended school events.

'I can't see it.'

They had searched all over the JR station, but found no sign of Shohei's poster.

'In that case, we need to try the subway,' Miho's father said in a low voice.

'Subway?'

'We can try other JR stations on the way back to Jujo, but let's go to the subway now.'

The subway section of Shibuya Station was somewhere that Miho had wanted to avoid if possible. It was a huge multi-floor maze, that right now would be thronging with rush-hour commuters heading for home. The crowds alone were exhausting.

'Mum, are you okay? Can you still walk?'

Miho's concern drew a slightly bigger smile from Tomoko. 'I'm fine.'

'Let's go to the floor with the ticket gate first,' said her father in what was, for him, an unusually commanding tone.

'Okay,' Miho acquiesced. After all, he was her father.

Miho watched her parents' backs as they headed for the subway stairs. They had been so adamantly against her marrying Shohei, yet here they were doing their best to find his poster. She decided that even if they didn't succeed, today had been worth it just for this.

There was still no sign of the poster in the passageway near the shops and ticket gate.

'We'll have to buy a platform ticket,' Miho's father murmured.

'It's all right. We've done enough. I'll try another station some other day and when I find it, I'll let you both know.'

'But we've come this far. You'll regret it if we don't take a last look around here,' said her father, and went to wait in line at the ticket machine to buy platform tickets.

'Your father seems to be taking his mother's advice,' Tomoko said, as she and Miho waited.

'What advice?'

'To get a bit more actively involved, since this concerns his daughter's future partner. Otherwise, he'll regret it later.'

'Did she really say that?'

'She also said there'll be fewer and fewer chances for spending family time with you.'

'Fewer and fewer . . .'

'If you marry and have children, it might be our last chance to have any kind of input in your decisions.'

'I don't believe it.'

Tomoko smiled sadly.

'Right then, let's go.' Miho's father returned with the tickets. 'I think this might be the first time I've ever used a platform ticket,' he said.

'Come to think of it, me too,' said Miho, her grandmother's words echoing in her head. She met her mother's eyes at last and they both smiled. They were family after all.

'Let's go to the Fukutoshin Line on the bottom floor first. We can work our way up from there.'

They took two long rides in a lift, going deep underground.

'I've never been on this line before, it must be a long way down,' said Miho's mother, turning to look at Miho and her husband in surprise.

'The Fukutoshin line is the most recently built. They probably ran out of space higher up.'

A train was arriving just as they reached the platform, which quickly filled with people.

'Sorry. I'll run ahead and look. If I find it, I'll come back. You two come after me slowly.'

Miho went to race off, but her mother stopped her. 'It's not safe to run here. Let's stay together. We can take our time and check both sides of the platform as we go.'

Her father nodded in agreement.

'Okay then. Thank you, I'm sorry about this.' Miho was apologetic.

Halfway down the platform, they found it. As if in a dream,

the object of their search appeared, about ten metres ahead. Miho could tell straight away it was Shohei's. She felt the same leap in her chest as she had the first time she laid eyes on his work.

'What's wrong?' her mother asked, noticing that Miho had sped up.

'I think that's it,' she said, pointing as they drew closer. It was indeed the poster for the classical duo that Shohei had wrote about in his email.

'This is it?'

'Yeah, I'm positive.'

The three stood straight on facing the poster. It was much bigger than Miho had expected. The picture was painted in tiny golden dots on a background black as night. It looked like a star, but on closer examination could also be a woman's face in profile and the moon. Her lightly crimson-tinted lips resembled a heart, floating in the black of night. Details for the concert's time, place and the name of the duo were all subtly inscribed in the same gold colour as the picture.

It's really lovely, thought Miho. *Simple at first glance, but quite exquisite.*

'I wonder if that's lacquer,' her father murmured.

'What?'

'It looks like a straightforward picture, but could be an arrangement of a photo taken of a specially commissioned piece of lacquerware.'

Now that he mentioned it, Miho noticed a cloud-like streak near the edge that could be a lacquerware gloss.

'You're right. You've got a good eye, Dad.'

'It's certainly very intricate,' her mother commented, sounding impressed.

Miho's father put a hand on her shoulder. 'Let's ask him over and tell us how he made it.'

'What? Are you sure?' She looked at her mother. Tomoko stared at the poster with a small crease between her brows.

'Whatever we decide about any marriage, let's at least do it after meeting him. I have a feeling we might regret it otherwise. That's the kind of work this is,' said her father.

Miho's mother eventually gave a small nod.

The following weekend, Shohei visited the Mikuriya house, wearing a suit.

'Well spotted,' he said in surprise, when Miho's father pointed out his observation. 'You're right. I had a piece of lacquerware made, photographed it, then arranged the photo using software. To be honest, it was an expensive, time-consuming process. My boss was pretty unhappy, and senior colleagues said I should have done the whole thing with software, but I didn't think that would produce the right kind of depth so I dug my heels in.' Shohei leaned forward as he spoke, pleased at his hard work having been recognised, but then abruptly remembered where he was – in the living room of his girlfriend's family home – and smiled shyly before taking a sip of the tea that Tomoko offered him.

'Did you study those … ah, techniques at university?' Tomoko asked, sitting down beside her husband. It was apparent that she was making an effort to get to know Shohei, even if she didn't approve of him as a suitable partner for her daughter.

'Yes, they taught us all the basics there. The last few months I've also learned a huge amount since starting at the company. They have state-of-the-art technology, and my colleagues are highly skilled. I'm really learning a lot,' Shohei replied crisply. Though he must have been aware that Miho's parents knew about the student loan, and of their opposition to a marriage, he sounded undaunted, almost as if he were even enjoying the conversation.

'It sounds like a good place to work.'

Miho was impressed. Fancy her father speaking; he was usually a man of few words.

'A teacher I once had used to say that there are many things you will never learn until you start getting paid. It's true, I've found. My workplace is strict, busy, and the money's not good, but they're passionate about teaching, and the work is rewarding. The people are good, too, which helps.'

Her father nodded and huffed in agreement.

'I'm just repeating my teacher again, but he used to say that a job can have good pay, good work or good people. If you can tick the box for any one of these, you'll survive, but if all three come up short then quit or you'll fall apart. I can tick two out of three, so I think I'll be all right.' Shohei scratched his head with a laugh, and Miho's parents laughed along with him.

Memories flooded through Miho's mind as she sat beside him. The time she bought a dress at a shop in Shinjuku when she and Shohei had first started seeing each other. After returning home she had noticed that the hem of the dress was coming undone and immediately taken it back, only to have the shop assistant bluntly refuse to let her return it. Shohei then stepped in and negotiated with the assistant to accept the return without causing an argument or anger. He really came through for her that day.

His language and manner had become more polished since starting work at the design firm, which made him seem even more reliable and solid. More often than not their dates involved hanging out at each other's place, so Miho had not really noticed this public side of him so much.

'Do you know what,' said her mother, turning to her husband, then Shohei, 'I'd like to ask you for lunch, but I was in hospital recently so I'm not my usual self.'

'Oh, I heard from Miho. I'm sorry to intrude at such a time.'

'Not at all, we invited you. Well, anyway we discussed ordering in some sushi or eel, so I wonder which you would prefer, Shohei? If you don't like fish, we could get something else. That would be fine, too.'

Shohei looked at Miho.

She nodded. 'Feel free.'

'In that case, is sushi all right?'

'Yes, I'll order some sushi.'

The conversation, and questions, continued to flow even once the sushi had been delivered from a neighbourhood shop. What clubs had Shohei been in at middle school and high school? What made him decide to major in art? And, on his part, what was Miho like as a child?

'This is homemade soup, isn't it, Mrs Mikuriya?' Shohei said, cupping the bowl in his hand.

'Oh, yes. That at least, I made.'

The soup contained an open clam that could perhaps be taken as a small token of celebration from a mother on the occasion of the first visit to the house of the man who her daughter might marry.

'It's delicious. The stock is very good.'

'I usually use granulated powder to make the soup broth, but as we have a guest today, I used kombu kelp to make it from scratch.'

'Wow. My mum is a terrible cook. It's the first time I've had anything like this outside of a restaurant.'

Miho sensed a slight air of tension between her parents when Shohei brought up his family.

'Miho has mentioned . . .' Tomoko set down her chopsticks and sat up straight.

'About the student loan?' Shohei also put down his chopsticks, having almost finished his sushi.

'Yes.'

Miho noticed that her mother had hardly eaten. Despite her calm appearance, in reality she was probably nervous. 'You talked about this with Dad, didn't you?'

Her parents looked at each other and nodded.

'Mum, we don't have to discuss this now.'

'Yes, Miho, we do.'

'It's fine. I understand,' Shohei interjected. 'I know you must be worried. It's natural, because it's a lot of money. For my part, I believe that it is my responsibility to repay the debt as my education was the cause of it.' Shohei bowed his head. 'I'm sorry. If you object to me because of it, I cannot blame you. But may I ask you to wait a while? Even if I am not able to marry right now, I would like to continue seeing Miho, and at the same time try and find a way to repay the debt, or deal with it somehow.'

Then Shohei told them of his plan, which he had obviously been thinking about for some time. 'I haven't stopped thinking about this. I thought that I could move somewhere cheaper to cut back on living expenses, that would help me repay a fair bit. And I also asked at work if they were okay with me taking another job on my days off. They're fine with me finding a part-time job, so I can start paying back the money.'

Miho's parents looked at each other again.

'You would do all that?'

'Yes, I would. Though I am really sorry about making you wait, Miho.'

Miho's father looked at his wife, as if to ask her permission. 'It's all right, isn't it, Tomoko?'

She gave a small nod.

'Actually, we have an idea, too.'

'What?' Miho's heart raced, as if she was about to hear bad news. Her mother looked at her directly with a small reassuring shake of her head.

'We've been discussing this a lot, too. And discussing it with my mother, Miho's grandmother, as well. As a result, we have decided that we can give five hundred thousand yen to Miho as a wedding gift, and you can borrow the remaining five million from my mother. Then you could repay the money to the association as a lump sum, and for the next ten years pay back my mother with an interest rate of one per cent. Which would come to roughly 43,800 yen per month. Of course, you will have to write an IOU. If you both continue to work, and are able to pay back the money over ten years, it will reduce the impact on your future, don't you think?'

'Father.' It had been a long time since Miho had heard her father speak so assertively and at such length.

'More than anything, it would be a waste to pay almost two million yen in interest. But if you can repay the loan in ten years, you'll be free of it before you have a real need for money, even if you have children in the next few years.'

'If you do have children, or something happens to your grandmother, we can revisit the repayment amounts at that time,' Tomoko added.

'But why would you do such a thing for me?' Shohei exclaimed, too surprised to even say thanks or express his appreciation. 'Why would you put yourselves out like that for me – a stranger?'

'Because we're family. Miho is our precious daughter, and we want her to be happy,' Tomoko said heatedly. 'I'll be honest. This money – the five-hundred-thousand-yen gift and money from my mother-in-law – it's no trifling sum to us. We have need of it too, and things will be quite tight. Please understand that. But also understand this: we want you to make Miho happy.'

'Thank you, Father, Mother.' Miho bowed her head.

'You should thank your grandmother,' her mother said. 'She was the one to suggest it.'

'Miho has probably told you about my family. I've never received such love from my parents. It's possible I may behave ineptly in some way with Miho in future, but if I do, I ask you for your guidance and help to do the right thing.' Shohei stood up and bowed deeply. 'Thank you very much. I'm truly sorry about all this. I will never forget my debt of gratitude to you.'

'We're counting on you.'

Through her tears, Miho could see that Shohei's eyes were wet too.

And that is how the matter of the student loan was settled for now. We will be repaying the money for the next ten years. I am sure it is going to be long and difficult. Sometimes, I get scared thinking about it. We're trying to rent a place as close as possible to my grandmother Funeko, and on each repayment day, we plan to visit her and hand it over in person.

She is surprisingly casual about all this, though. According to her, 'It's hard to secure 1% interest anywhere these days.' That's my grandmother for you, always so positive.

If you're wondering how I came round to the idea, this is how I see it. Everything in life is an opportunity for experience, and being in debt is just one more. I will be giving you all the nitty-gritty in this blog on how we are going with our loan repayments, so please stay tuned!

There are so many things in life that we have no control over. Age, illness, gender, time. Some kinds of debt are like that too, I believe. So wouldn't it be strange then if those of us with debt couldn't be happy? Am I wrong to think this? Money and economising are meant to help people be happy. They're not an end in themselves. That's what my grandmother told me, and now I truly believe it.